UNFORGIVABLE

A NOVEL

PHILIPPE DJIAN

TRANSLATED FROM THE FRENCH BY
EUAN CAMERON

SIMON & SCHUSTER
New York · London · Toronto · Sydney

Simon & Schuster
1230 Avenue of the Americas
New York, NY 10020

First Simon & Schuster hardcover edition March 2010

SIMON & SCHUSTER and colophon are registered trademarks
of Simon & Schuster, Inc.

For information about special discounts for bulk purchases,
please contact Simon & Schuster Special Sales at
1-866-506-1949 or business@simonandschuster.com.

The Simon & Schuster Speakers Bureau can bring authors
to your live event. For more information or to book an event
contact the Simon & Schuster Speakers Bureau at
1-866-248-3049 or visit our website at www.simonspeakers.com.

Designed by Kyoko Watanabe

Manufactured in the United States of America

10   9   8   7   6   5   4   3   2   1

Library of Congress Cataloging-in-Publication Data
Djian, Philippe, date.
  [Impardonnables. English]
  Unforgivable : a novel / Philippe Djian ; translated from the French by Euan
Cameron.
    p. cm.
  1. Pays Basque (France)—Fiction. 2. Families—France—Pays Basque—Fiction.
I. Cameron, Euan. II. Title.
  PQ2664.J5I4713 2009
  843'.914—dc22
                                                            2009051130

ISBN 978-1-4391-6441-9
ISBN 978-1-4391-7018-2 (ebook)

UNFORGIVABLE

I KNEW VERY WELL THAT SHE WASN'T THERE. I WAS listening to the wonderfully plaintive, husky voice of Patti Smith singing "Pastime Paradise" as I watched Alice's plane coming in to land, cumbersome and shimmering in the still warm, orange-tinged, late-summer sunshine, knowing full well that she wasn't on board.

I did not normally have this kind of premonition—something I was almost blamed for—but that morning I had warned Judith that our daughter would not be on the plane and that it would be better to wait before ordering the meat. What would be the point of that? I had not known how to explain. Judith maintained that she would at least have phoned us.

I had shrugged my shoulders. My wife was probably right. Barely a minute later, however, I became convinced once more that Alice would not be there.

When he disembarked from the plane, Roger announced that she had not been home for two days. I said nothing and hugged the twin girls, who did not appear in the least bothered by their mother's absence and were making a point of yawning.

"You're having marvelous weather," he said to me. "It will do them good."

As a rule, children arriving from the city were pale and often had large rings under their eyes, and these two little creatures were no exception.

In a confidential tone, out of the girls' hearing, Roger made it clear to me that he'd had enough. There was no need for him to say so. Nobody, on seeing him, could think that this chap looked well.

"Mmm . . . ," I muttered, "what is it this time? A film? A play?"

"It doesn't matter what it's to do with, Francis. I couldn't care less whether it's for this reason or that. I've had enough, Francis. She can go to hell."

Without any question, he had been patient, but all I could do was to encourage him to hang on—aware, as far as I was concerned, of the rapidly approaching specter of having to look after the twins should the relationship explode, a situation that Judith and I had experienced two years previously when they had set off on a trip together in order to start afresh on a new footing.

At the age of sixty, there were certain things I was no longer prepared to discuss. I longed for peace. I wanted to read books, listen to music, go for early morning walks in the mountains or on the beach. Looking after children, even if they were my own flesh and blood as Judith never hesitated to remind me, scarcely interested me anymore. I had taken care of Alice and her sister in their time and I seemed to have exhausted the entire range of experiences potentially capable of stimulating the youthful old fellow I had become today; my time was precious, even if I was writing virtually nothing any longer.

And so it was that later on, at the end of the meal, when I was given the task of taking the girls down to the seashore before they began wreaking havoc in the garden from top to bottom, I was unable to prevent myself from grimacing, for I had been on the very point of settling upstairs, in the pleasant shade of my office, with my laptop on my knees, that is to say in my armchair, with my hands folded behind my head—oh how I should like death to come and take me unawares in such a posture, if possible, instead of in a hospital with tubes up my nose—and then everything fell apart, toppling into the sea, as if from the thirty-sixth floor, it all collapsed. Thanks to two little eight-year-old girls deserted by their mother. I gave them each a hard candy and told them they were to wait for me outside while I tried to call Alice, who did not answer.

"Now, Roger, believe me, I'm on your side. I know her. But what is it, two days . . . ? Forty-eight hours? Well . . . she's done worse, hasn't she? There may not be any need to panic . . ."

My words were meant to be reassuring. I personally had no cause to be anxious, as far as Alice was concerned, just because of two miserable days without news, other than that certainty I'd had when I woke up that she would not be getting off the plane. I didn't know how to interpret the intuition, but I could not get it out of my mind. Alice sometimes disappeared for an entire week. So why should these two days arouse such a vague uneasiness in me?

"I bet you we'll have some news before the weekend is over," I added eventually.

There was very little chance of my being wrong. Alice never lost her wits completely. Had she not married a banker? God knows she went around with street musicians, layabouts, and drug addicts at the time, but she must have had her head firmly screwed onto her shoulders to pick a banker from out of the pack. "You gave us one hell of a fright," I told her on the day of her wedding. Her only response was to look daggers at me.

The following day, Roger spoke to me about some marks Alice had on her thighs and her breasts. I hadn't slept very well. The twins had had nightmares and Roger had given them four mg of Rohypnol on my advice. "Marks, you say?" I frowned as I fingered some overripe mangoes at my usual greengrocer. "What do you mean, marks, Roger?"

I thought about this throughout the afternoon. I wondered whether she would ever try to protect me from worrying about her. Things did not seem to be going very well. Roger tried to call her several times, without success.

As dusk fell, the breeze picked up and Roger helped me put away the parasol and anything else that might be blown away beneath the dark and rumbling sky, other than the bougainvillea flowers that the gusts of wind beat back sharply against the wall of the house and beheaded. The beam from the lighthouse swept across the vast and impressive dark clouds.

Judith returned just before the storm. From San Sebastián. The gale had been following her all the way from San Sebastián, she said. There had been flashes of heat lightning during the afternoon.

The twins were as alike as two peas in a pod, but the one who was a fraction younger, Anne-Lucie, jumped to her feet and declared that she was going to put on her swimsuit. A promise was a promise. Outside, all along the front, clusters of whitish foam were being blown up by the rough sea and were smashing into the palm trees that lined the beach. You had to shout to make yourself heard. Roger seemed completely befuddled.

Few people came to the swimming pool in the evenings—on that particular day, there was nobody—and we sat down beside the bay windows that looked out over the choppy sea. The view was splendid—it was as if we were sitting at the bow of an ocean liner, hurtling through the spray.

Judith was in a quandary. "To answer your question,

Roger, I believe Alice is an intelligent person. She's past that age when you do something just for the sake of it. Let's trust her. She needs a breath of fresh air, if you like. It's vital as far as she is concerned. Why should we necessarily see anything bad in that?"

I kept an eye on Anne-Lucie, who was a long time coming to the surface, while at the same time nodding my head and agreeing with Judith.

"Am I wrong to see anything bad in it?" Roger yelped. *"Am I wrong, Judith?"*

Our eyes met. I have never claimed that my daughter was a saint. Her indiscretions were public knowledge. News travels fast in those circles. I did not really see that I had anything to feel guilty about.

"Please don't look at me like that. I reckon I've given my children a good education. I've devoted countless days and nights to it. To teaching them the difference between good and evil. Months and years, Roger. I'm not responsible for anything, my friend."

I stood up to help Anne-Lucie out of the pool after she appeared to have sprained her wrist. I left her in charge of her father so that I could go for a swim.

I was about to be sixty. The doctors advised swimming as much as possible and eating healthily in order to live a long life. I could cope with both instructions easily.

◆

After a week, we decided to inform the police. The spring tides had begun. Roger scarcely opened his mouth anymore. Every possible telephone call had been made, we had questioned her friends and the friends of her friends, and even others, who certainly weren't very pleased, but nobody knew a thing, nobody had seen her or spoken to her these past ten days, nobody knew her whereabouts.

Judith set off for San Sebastián once more and so I spent almost a week on my own with Roger and the girls. I wondered whether it was his intention to starve himself to death. He was only just thirty years old and was already beginning to lose his hair.

"I'm not saying it's easy to earn one's living, Roger. I'm saying that it's easy to lose a woman. There's a slight difference. Opening your eyes and seeing that she's no longer there, that you've lost her."

Sometimes I left him in a particular spot and found him again an hour or two later in the very same place, doing absolutely nothing, and half asleep. He probably called that struggling.

We spent a whole morning with the police investigators, long enough in any case to realize we should expect nothing from this quarter; these men and women went back home every evening and confronted their own problems, their partners, their children, their neighbors. Even though they appeared to be concerned, you didn't feel they were ready to leap out of their armchairs to bring Alice back to us.

I, too, was overcome with anxiety. Time dragged on in its dull and superficial way. I went out with the twins. When we returned home, we would sometimes discover their father stretched out on the sofa; lively was hardly the word.

I did the cooking; Judith had had to extend her visit to the other side of the Spanish frontier in order to complete the sale of a seafront property for which prices had soared in recent months. The sky was still overcast. Alice. My daughter. I thought of her constantly. I could see entire scenes in my mind's eye. Cooking, for example. I had taught her to cook. During the two years we had lived together—between the accident and the day that I married Judith—I had tried to alleviate our ordeal by teaching her certain basic recipes, an omelet with chilies, for example, or a fricassee of flambéed kidneys. We were able to talk. We had succeeded in keeping ourselves afloat. A real achievement.

I hired a detective. Roger suggested sharing the costs, but I refused. I chose a woman, a certain Anne-Marguerite Lémo, who lived half a mile from my home and whom I had known at school.

From the information I had been able to glean locally, it was clear that Anne-Marguerite was the best in her field. I called on her straightaway to tell her about our problem.

It had been a good forty years since we had last seen one another; we swapped past memories and spent a little while bringing each other up to date with our respective lives. She had a son. Her husband had died of a heart attack. For a private detective who was no longer young, her figure was still quite shapely.

Anne-Marguerite had heard about the accident in which my wife and one of my daughters had been killed in the autumn of 1996. The newspapers had devoted a lot of space to it. I accepted her condolences and explained what had happened.

I gave her two thousand euros to start with. She accepted only half, giving the excuse that we had been good friends years ago. She was exaggerating. Everybody screwed everyone else at that time. She conscientiously took a few notes as the rain fell outside the window of the office she shared with an insurance company in the center of town.

"I can't wait to find Alice," she said as she reached out her hand to me.

At last, a little enthusiasm. At last, someone who gave me an open smile. She shook hands vigorously.

Anne-Marguerite Lémo. My near-neighbor. What else was this world but a tiny village full of hilarious coincidences?

Roger returned to Paris a few days later. I didn't try to stop him, quite the reverse, I had even encouraged him to go. I much preferred looking after the twins to his gloomy company—which never failed to fuel my anxiety.

We agreed to keep each other informed about the slightest bit of information and I went with him to the airport after having given him two Xanax tablets and a friendly pat on the back.

There was no better grandmother than Judith for the little girls—they adored her—and so I was fortunate enough not to be the one whose duty it was to read the bedtime story. When Judith was there.

I didn't know whether she was in the process of selling the entire La Concha Bay, but we didn't see much of her. When she came home, she listened to our news. When she left again, she gave me various instructions.

She maintained that she was snowed under with work. Any kind of sexual relationship between us was more or less nonexistent.

I read *Bridget Jones's Diary* to them up until the moment a deep silence descended and directed me to tiptoe out of the room, holding my breath.

Once night had fallen and I was alone, I could not resist the urge to ring Anne-Marguerite, knowing very well that if she had not called me it was because there was nothing new to report, but she never seemed irritated or disturbed by my foolish phone calls and appeared, on the contrary, full of concern. I felt grateful to her. As one hour followed another, I felt the need to talk about Alice. Uttering her name protected her, it seemed to me.

The first mention of her disappearance in the press made my blood run cold, and my phone started ringing continuously. People in these circles were hungry for news and half the actors and actresses in the country—I kept the other half waiting—appeared determined to wail into my ear for ages. The sky was low. Each time I put down the phone, I caught the little girls gazing at me and I cursed myself for having mentioned their mother's disappearance in their presence—what was I thinking of—until the moment my phone started vibrating again.

In the afternoon, I switched off the vibrator—I had turned off the ringing sound some time ago. After a while, all those sighs, all those tears fused into one dull and gloomy lament that I could do without.

I prepared a sumptuous sort of afternoon snack, so as to excuse myself for having forgotten their midday meal, which consisted of a large bowl of cereal and puffed rice; I had instinctively stocked the cupboards while they were there and bought a supply of low-fat milk as well.

Anne-Marguerite's son was in prison. She told me about this as I was preparing for the tea party by flipping some pancakes. She shrugged her shoulders. A burglary that had been bungled. I looked at her incredulously for a moment, as my empty frying pans began to smoke; unless one enjoys having a rough time of it, the lot of a father or a mother is really the worst that can happen to one, isn't it? Examples abound, do they not?

"I thought of you as I opened my newspaper," she continued. "It may well be that you're in for a difficult time, Francis."

It certainly was. With or without the press. With or without friends. With or without the telephone.

My daughter's past, along with the inquiries made day after day, led the police to believe that it was an elopement, or the latest in the line of sordid incidents with which her professional career and love life had been scattered.

This did not mean, they pointed out, that they were stopping their search, but I must understand that since all leads had come to nothing, and in the absence of any new information, the investigations, at this juncture, could advance no further. Would they continue to search for her? Of course they would continue to search. I would gain nothing from behaving unpleasantly. Who enjoyed going around in circles? Who did not wish for a happy and speedy conclusion to this business? What policeman did not seriously want to bring my daughter back to me safe and sound?

The inspector who had made these comments to me slightly increased my anxiety, for I had not yet envisaged the possibility that my daughter's *life* was in danger. "I never imagined this for a second, Anne-Mar. Not consciously, at least. How would I have had the strength to imagine such a thing? How can you imagine something that could destroy you?"

Anne-Marguerite nodded. For three days, she had been

in Paris making inquiries, and she had come back totally empty-handed. I began to feel really isolated. The presence of the twins—whom Roger, still apparently off his rocker, was taking back home—made the ordeal less difficult, but the only moments that gave me a real breathing space were when Anne-Marguerite came to see us and took over from me, for in this way I benefited freely from their presence a little, and from the invigorating sound of their conversation, without being required to join in.

It was to Judith—to her symbolic absence, her lack of concern about supporting me—that I owed this painful situation.

Ten years of marriage had left us both punch-drunk. Strangely groggy. Incapable of explaining lucidly what it was that had happened to us. As if anesthetized. We were incapable of expressing it, but we did not pretend to be unaware of it.

She went away quite readily. More and more frequently. It was not uncommon for her to disappear now for several days and I was satisfied with her explanations; I did not seek to know the details of how she spent her time. I was amazed to discover how insurmountable was the wall that stood between us. Looking into one another's eyes no longer served any purpose. When she set off, I wished her a safe journey. She promised to call me. And she did so—without losing out on her fixed rate of charges, of course.

Be that as it may, leaving me alone with the twins was

a really dirty trick. In the tense, worried condition I was in. But it was not for me to tell her so.

That evening, she had dined in a cider house with some Spanish estate agents and had been unable to extricate herself any earlier.

"You shouldn't have telephoned to say that you were on your way," I said. "They were waiting for you."

"I nearly ran over a porcupine."

"I had a devil of a time getting them to go to sleep. After your phone call."

"It delayed me. I had to make sure it got across the road safely. Didn't I do the right thing?"

The doorbell rang. Anne-Marguerite wanted to walk away immediately, imagining that she was disturbing us, but I insisted and introduced them to one another.

Anne-Marguerite, or Anne-Mar, whom I now called A.-M.—that was what her son called her—had come to see whether all was well with the twins, and I could see a mixture of gratitude and irritation—just a fleeting hint—in Judith's expression at my detective friend's remark.

At the age of fifty, Judith still belonged to the desirable category, no question of it—whereas I was not sure of being so any longer. In fact, I had made the terrible mistake of wanting her to replace Johanna, Alice's mother, and look where my madness had led us, to this uncontrollable and disastrous distancing—this gradual and deadly struggle—which Judith and I, hypnotized and numbed by the progress of such failure, watched happening.

A.-M. appeared to be upset by my stories, but she herself knew how sorrow could make one foolish—I had to believe her—and she therefore refused to be too critical of me.

It was twenty-one days since Alice had disappeared. I continued to take my daily dose of a hundred sixty mg of pantoprazole to control the burning in my stomach.

A.-M. had gone back to Paris to explore new leads, but without any success.

"What do you think? Tell me if you think it's a lost cause, A.-M. I prefer to know. Listen, if you have discovered something, the slightest thing, tell me. Even if it's only a hunch."

"Nothing is lost, Francis. I believe she has been abducted, as I've told you. I'm convinced she's alive."

I was very glad when she said that: *I'm convinced she's alive.*

I had called Roger. I had allowed him to moan and wail, then I had asked him to come and collect his daughters. Why? Did I have to provide him with explanations? "Because I'm no longer twenty, Roger. Of course I love them. Of course I adore them. That's not the problem." Then Judith had called me from Madrid, an hour later, to tell me how heartless I was. The nerve of that woman!

But I hadn't given in. Roger arrived by plane the following day and we had scarcely exchanged more than a few words while the girls packed their suitcases. I had not found him as distraught as I had imagined I would after listening to him whining and moaning down the phone. Apart from the lines of bitterness around his lips, he did not look too bad—he was naturally pale.

At the front of the house, the eucalyptus trees were losing their bark. I was annoyed with him for having forced me to ask him to come and collect his children. I gazed at the swaying Chinese lanterns that the girls had hung on the lower branches for the party they had organized the previous day and from which I had only barely recovered. Olga, my daughter who had died, used to make very pretty ones, of different shapes, when she was their age. She was someone who was particularly gifted with her hands.

Once they had finally left and set off for the airport, I felt a bit low and wondered whether I had made a mistake. How silent it suddenly was. How empty.

What a void I felt around me.

I made a fire—just for the sake of the crackling, and the flickering dance of the flames from one wall to the other— and I settled down with the letters of Flannery O'Connor, who generally proved to be a good cure. Dusk was falling. The Spanish coast was already steeped in darkness and high above the garden the first stars were twinkling. But Alice's disappearance made me feel dejected.

Helplessness was the worst torture of all.

A.-M. knew this. A.-M. understood this. She was kind enough to come by. She had probably realized that Judith and I no longer enjoyed the perfect love life and that I needed a bit of support, given the storms that I was going through and the gales that were blowing across my path.

"She's still a very beautiful woman," she said. "Superb breasts."

"True. And to my knowledge, she has never breast-fed. That's the reason for that."

I got up to mix us some Bloody Marys—it was a drink she was fond of.

She had just come back from the prison, from one of those distressing visits to her son, after which, in a ludicrous reversal of roles, it would become my turn to offer her my shoulder. I knew everything now about Jérémie Lémo. I could recognize him in a crowd without ever having met him.

On the day I accompanied A.-M. to the prison visiting room, I was momentarily flabbergasted by the resemblance between the original and the portrait his mother had painted for me.

As for him, he stared at me suspiciously. However much he frowned, he seemed so much younger than his supposed twenty-five years.

A.-M. maintained that her son was responsible for every single white hair on her head. He had just treated his mother like a whore after having refused to shake my hand,

and as a result she and I, feeling rather piqued, were retracing our steps back to my car, in the lee of a west wind that had blown up from the sea.

We folded back the sunroof. When all was said and done, the notion that her son should have thought we were lovers brought smiles to our faces.

A.-M. was as old as I was. What would be the point in my taking a mistress who was as old as me? Even if my dreams were filled with lively young women, every one of them more attractive than the other . . . and by the way, while on the subject, the latest Philip Roth had depressed me and left me feeling half-dead for days afterward.

A.-M. was not repellent in any way. It was simply that her body no longer sent out any signal, at least not in my direction. Somewhere, buried deep down, the batteries appeared to be dead. But let's be quite clear, that did not mean she was ugly or repellent, merely old.

Her features were regular. In certain photographs dating from the seventies, she looked like Juliette Gréco—with her original nose.

Judith very much enjoyed selling houses. Ten years previously, she had sold me the one in which we live today, and

I can attest to her skill at conducting property transactions. Like A.-M. in matters that required investigation, Judith was the best in her field. All the most attractive deals went through her hands. She knew the area like the back of her hand and she was very proficient at her job. She spoke Russian and Spanish. Characters used to arrive from the Urals and the steppes with suitcases full of cash—which I sometimes had to keep in our house for a few days, thereby risking having my throat slit—and she did the deal in the buyer's language—Russian made her garrulous—a service that no other agency offered, and one that made it an absolute must for our brothers from the East who came to these parts in quest of a little calm and quiet, to breathe the pure ocean air and enjoy the spray of the sea. The Russians *blew* their money happily. The mayor and his counselors had traveled as far as Saint Petersburg to sing the praises of the region and to point out the benefits of settling there, investing, etc. As a result, Judith had no time left for me.

Nothing obliged her to fill her appointment diary to the hilt. But we were passing through the most difficult period since we were married and we had agreed to stand back a little. Property was rocketing in San Sebastián.

When she thought of it, she brought me back cigarettes. She handed me a carton and said to me: "You know, that woman . . . I've nothing against her, but . . ."

"No, wait . . . I know what you're driving at, it's just . . ."

"On the contrary, far be it from me to suggest that . . ."

"She has done everything that was possible. I know that.

There's absolutely nothing to blame her for. I know she's done everything. She really is very good. Believe me."

Although it wasn't yet very pronounced, the tension between us did not ease off. I don't know whether it indicated she was having an affair, or merely frustration; there were throngs of glossy-haired *hombres* on the other side of the border.

"Do you think the police have done any better?" I added. "They've made no progress at all."

Because she understood what I was going through better than anyone else and was aware of my previous tragedy, she was able to treat me tactfully in spite of my occasional bad moods.

It had taken me some time to convince myself that no woman was going to replace the one I had lost. The momentum of my recovery had been akin to continental drift, so much so that everything—the essential things, at least—had deteriorated before my very eyes without my realizing it.

Quite simply, I believe I had made her lose heart.

These types of thoughts went through my mind now that my life was starting to collapse and that I was no longer in a state to do anything about anything; the appalling disappearance of my daughter had affected me like a paralyzing poison with every passing day. Was it possible for a man to lose his two daughters in the space of twelve years? Could fate dog one like this?

Merely thinking about it made me shiver. Nevertheless, I could see only too well that any reasonably sensible woman—and Judith was certainly that—would not wish to come back from work to find a creature like me and endure his depressing company. I could easily understand that she would be in no hurry to return home and spend the evening with me.

I had made her lose heart. It was as simple as that.

I should probably even congratulate myself that she had not yet left me. I more or less thought as much, anyway. Even though I would go out and practice a few breathing exercises on the seafront, I was unable to fill my lungs. Occasionally, she came and massaged my shoulders.

I was obliged to phone Roger, otherwise, he didn't call me. "I want you to call me, do you hear? Even if you've got no news, I want you to call me. You can easily do that, can't you? Even if it's just to tell me you've got no news, OK? It's all very well to sigh, but do as I tell you."

The police eventually admitted that a month without news was not a very good sign. "And you came just to tell me that?" I asked. "Both of you."

I hardly slept anymore, except for brief periods. My nights were split into a dozen phases in which I slept and woke alternately. As a result, I would fall asleep three or four times during the day, nodding off no matter where, in the supermarket, or in the bar, or in the newspaper shop.

People knew what was troubling me, and some of the shopkeepers offered me a chair and sympathized with me as my head slumped forward onto my chest. It was as if half the town was trying to pat me on the back. When they had heard about the deaths of my wife and my daughter, they had had masses said for their intentions. With choirs; some of them had even come down from the mountains especially.

The majority of them had followed Alice's career—such a pretty girl, such a good actress, how proud her father must be—and not a day went by without some woman coming up to me and reciting my daughter's entire curriculum vitae, without dwelling on certain less savory episodes, of course.

"Why don't you go for a drive in your car?" Judith suggested. "Go and do your shopping in Spain . . ."

"What do you expect me to buy in Spain?" I replied.

Furthermore, I had no desire to drive. I wasn't hungry either. If I was alone, I didn't eat. I didn't think of it. If she knew I was alone, A.-M. would break off from her current investigations and bring sandwiches, hot dogs, Chinese or Indian meals, Italian, Greek, or even Japanese food, it didn't really matter, it was all the same to me—to the extent that I was able to chew on a large lump of pickled ginger without batting an eyelid.

Since I scarcely spoke, it was A.-M. who took responsibility for the conversation. With a bit of luck, a sperm whale had been washed up on the beach. Another day, it was heroin, packed in one-kilo packets and cast up by the sea. Or the opening of a new golf course; the physical condition of the rugby team; an attack on a Guardia Civil garrison; gays who had been nabbed in the bushes at the foot of the lighthouse. Etc.

Otherwise, she talked to me about her son, Jérémie, who was going to be let out soon, and she was dreading the moment because the fellow was not easy. A real hothead, in my opinion.

A.-M. reckoned that it was necessary for the boy to see us together, for him to get used to my being with her when he came out, for him to digest the fact that his mother had found a friend—not a guy to sleep with.

On the day he was released, I went to collect him and things didn't go too badly, even though my mind was elsewhere. How long was it since Alice had disappeared? A month and a half? I was worn out. Jérémie looked at me as I drove toward the pine forests, bouncing over the speed bumps, then he eventually came out with the statement that, yes, it was beginning to be a long time, forty-five days.

I dropped him off outside his house. A.-M. appeared at the doorway. I waved and then drove off.

Jérémie had been arrested at a holdup at a service station. A stray bullet had hit the checkout operator full in the chest.

He had just done six years in jail. The thing he appeared to cherish most in the world was his CD player. He listened mainly to English rock music.

"Let me know when you're ready to look for a job," I said to him. "I may be able to give you a hand."

"Mind your own business," was his reply.

A.-M. wanted to allow him some time, a few weeks more, before raising the matter. He was her son. It was not for me to tell her what she should do; I didn't know either, being incapable of addressing my mind to anything other than Alice's disappearance.

One morning, as I was taking an early morning walk along the beach, clambering over the dunes in the pale, damp whiteness of dawn, I came across him, sitting on the sand. He was tossing a piece of wood for a puppy that had been hanging around the area for a few days.

"It must be tough. I wouldn't like to be in your shoes," I said to him.

On my way back, he was still there. The dog, too. Below him, a few small waves were encroaching on the sand, which was now gleaming in the morning light. It almost made you blink.

"How about going to have a coffee?" I suggested. I had an irresistible need to talk about Alice and, viewed in this light, the boy struck me as some vast uncharted territory.

I sat down opposite him. "You must have seen her in the last James Bond," I said to him. "Or else in *Voici*."

Occasionally, when I spoke about her, an image of the

two dead women attached itself to that of Alice, a sob would suddenly constrict my throat, and I would let out a sort of gurgling sound, or I burped, or else I doubled up.

Jérémie, unlike the others, did not bat an eyelid when a groan slipped from deep within me just as I was recalling the time when I was father to two grown-up girls and husband to an exceptional woman, Johanna, whom I had watched die in front of my very eyes. He did not ask me whether I was feeling all right. "Can I have some croissants?" he asked me. Some young men, dripping wet, emerged from the sea with their surfboards and sat down on the terrace to look at the ocean.

"Have whatever you like," I told him. "Far be it from me to disapprove of her conduct. Far be it from me, of course, to hold up my daughter as an example. But she could be granted extenuating circumstances, I reckon . . . no, don't you think so? And we know that milieu, don't we? We know that it's virtually impossible to escape from it unscathed. Wouldn't it be better just to take your child and chuck her out of the window? I'm joking."

I bent over toward the puppy to give it a lump of sugar, but Jérémie stopped me, claiming it wasn't good for its teeth. "They're his milk teeth, old friend. He's going to lose them," I said to him.

"I couldn't give a damn," he answered.

◆

At the time of her last visit, Alice had left behind a T-shirt on which was printed, in English, the inscription ABUSE OF POWER COMES AS NO SURPRISE, but it was too small for me.

It was washed and ironed, naturally, and it had a clean aroma of detergent. No trace of any smell of her, of course.

How could I have foreseen it all? Almost two months, now. Appalling.

I wasn't able to get my head through. It would reach down to my navel. Since I couldn't wear it, I had to make do with holding it in my hands.

The newspapers continued to mention her disappearance. Some of them were convinced she was still hiding in a private clinic, for a detox or God knows what, but I had telephoned every one of these establishments in turn, right at the very beginning, without the slightest success.

In this regard, at least, she was gradually becoming more reasonable. The twins had helped bring her down to earth more or less. Roger, too, had grown more mature. His wife's excesses amused him far less these days, he himself having vowed—after that dreadful evening when two of Anne-Lucie's fingers had rolled onto the carpet—that he would never touch anything again.

I longed for someone to get in touch and ask me to pay a ransom. I would willingly cross the town on foot and disappear into the forest with a suitcase full of banknotes; that was all I wanted, to be useful, but no one called me.

Judith was sleeping upstairs; she had begun yawning before supper was over. Her comings and goings exhausted her, as they did me. Her handbag, which I did not inspect in frantic detail, told me nothing about the sort of things she was up to, or anything of a possibly adulterous nature.

I wondered whether I was still capable of feeling anything, whether my brain's obsession with the disappearance of my daughter—the only one I had left—had not cut out everything else; I hoped that my search might arouse a hint of jealousy in me, but I felt nothing. I was barely conscious of what I was doing.

When she wasn't there, I was cross with her for leaving me alone, but when she returned home, her presence made me feel ill at ease. I was ashamed of the mindless state I was in, and I quickly averted my eyes. I mumbled sentences in which I did not understand a single word of what I was saying.

She was considering taking a room in San Sebastián if the buoyancy of the market continued.

"Good God," I said, "things are beginning to take a pretty turn."

"I don't know, Francis. I really don't know. Taking a room by the month would cost me less than a hotel. There's nothing more to it than that."

"And that's more than enough, I can assure you. If you could wait until I felt a little better, you would be doing me a kindness. You really would."

When she was around, I had to find a means of keeping myself busy, for I could immediately sense her gaze hanging over me. Especially in the evening, when she took advantage of the dim light to stare at me; I began to imagine that there were words inscribed on my forehead and that she was able to read them, and that was the last thing I wanted.

I was glad I had begun to smoke again. To make up for this, I walked a good deal. There was not a single book that took priority any longer, either to read or to write. I had time on my hands. Eventually, I would come across Jérémie at some time or other during the day. With that dog he appeared to have adopted and which was getting visibly fatter. It was very clever at running after bits of wood or pinecones.

"I can understand your position," I said to him. "But I'm doing what your mother asked me. It's up to you to accept or refuse. All I'm doing is passing on information to you."

"What the hell would I do in a casino?"

"I don't know. Croupier? How should I know?"

He whirled a stick in the air and the creature shot off at full speed, yapping as it went. "I'd rather die," he said. Impervious, the full moon lapped the sea, bathed the pine trees, bounced along the road, and then invited itself into the gardens.

Although she showed herself incapable of taking certain steps with regard to her son, A.-M. despaired at the lack of enthusiasm he showed about doing anything. She had probably hoped that I would back her, which was indeed the case, but the boy would not listen. I did not know the solution to this problem.

Eventually she sighed and admitted she couldn't cope. I had not particularly shone as a father. Not sufficiently to boast of any authority in the matter, and Jérémie's situation was well beyond my competence.

I should take care not to embroil myself too much, according to Judith. She had looked up the records on the Internet and the account of the holdup in which Jérémie had been involved elicited no sympathy for him as far as she was concerned. It mattered little who had fired. The checkout operator was dead. Because an idiot had decided to carry out a holdup at a service station. Didn't I think that was appalling?

Jérémie felt that he had not won Judith over, but he claimed that he could see things from her point of view and could understand her reservations about him.

He hardly dared come into the garden when she was at home and she scarcely encouraged him, but I did not want to interfere. I would go outside and stay to smoke a cigarette with him. We didn't talk much. We watched the dog running after the seagulls, which cried as they disappeared into the darkness. Judith asked me what was so important that I should desert her in this way and I didn't really know how to reply to her.

I had no reason to seek this boy's company apart from the fact that he was available at a time when I was going through one of the worst ordeals in my life.

He, too, had his problems, he wasn't in good shape, and this similarity—this inauspicious point in common— seemed to have the power to lighten certain burdens, to make them less painful to endure, both on one side and on the other. It's reassuring, is it not, to see that there are others as damaged as oneself, as mistreated, as lost, as broken as oneself?

A.-M. put me a little more in the picture, one morning, when she informed me that Jérémie's father had died in the boy's arms, a few days after the lad had celebrated his sixteenth birthday. The beginning of the problems that he had accumulated, up to his being thrown into a prison cell, stemmed from that moment.

I didn't imagine that Judith would consider that an excuse, I said to her in reply. We had risen at dawn to go and buy anchovies. A light veil of morning mist still covered the nearby mountaintops, which were piercing through the darkness. A.-M. gave a slight shrug of her shoulders; she was a mother first and foremost.

One of the mistakes I had made was my categorical refusal to have a child with Judith. She had taken it badly. She had taken it badly and I was now paying the consequences. I had hardened her heart. I was sometimes astonished by a certain coldness that she displayed—her attitude toward Jérémie was a perfect example—forgetting at the time (wretched, shameless amnesiac that I was) that I was the one responsible for it in the first place.

A.-M. had a family recipe for preserving anchovies that

consisted in covering them with table salt—not coarse salt, as it happens—with *fin sel,* in layer after layer, so that their flesh remained firm and red and, quite simply, succulent. There was an absolutely true story that went the rounds, according to which Hemingway, who had been awarded the Nobel Prize in the meantime, used to order them from A.-M.'s mother, right up to the time of his death, and she, in an average year, would send him fifty or so jars in boxes, the most recent of them to Ketchum, in Idaho, and that our Ernest—Ernesto as we called him here—had never settled with her for this last batch.

Confronted with five kilos of anchovies that had to be filleted, cleaned, washed, put in jars, etc., A.-M. left us to dash into town, for what purpose we weren't sure—she did not talk much about her work. I felt a certain fear when I noticed that Jérémie was still half asleep on his feet. On the way back, he had slept in the car. Coping with five kilos on my own did not exactly thrill me.

The dawn was rising. I made some coffee. Had I been like this when I was twenty-five? So feeble? "All right, let's roll up our sleeves," I said as I opened the shutters. Jérémie winced in the buttercup-yellow daylight. "Two months without news, Jérémie. It's almost two months, do you realize?"

I took hold of a fish, slit it open, gutted it, rinsed it

quickly under the tap, and then lay it on its bed of salt. I suggested to Jérémie that he do the same.

"It occurred one morning, twelve years ago. The same thing happened to a truck driver as happened to your father. A heart attack. I had got out of the car with Alice and we were walking over to the snack bar. We were setting off on vacation. They reckon the man had already lost consciousness when his tanker truck careered across the parking area like a cannonball, smashed into our car, and they were burned alive, Jérémie, they were burned in front of our very eyes. Both of them. Her mother and her sister. One mustn't forget that, before judging her. I tell you this so that you should understand. Look at Courtney Love. Who would blame her for going a bit too far from time to time? In any case, you know the story now. It's hard enough to cope in those circles in normal times. I can tell you that she fought. I can tell you she needed guts. It's not because I'm her father. Roger will tell you that she still wakes up with a start and in a sweat. In that world where everybody's on the lookout for the slightest weakness, for the slightest gaffe from the person opposite you . . ."

I noticed that he was staring at me. My cellar door closed over me once more. The heavy stone slab of my tomb took up its place again and reduced me to silence.

"Don't look like that," he said to me. "Not everything's lost."

◆

Roger brought the girls back for the All Saints' Day holiday. I thanked the heavens that Judith had returned to this side of the frontier and was able to greet them and embrace them like any self-respecting grandmother, and that she was determined to play her part as she should . . . Especially as she performed it extremely well. The girls refused to go to sleep without a last kiss from her.

When we collected them from the airport, Judith gave me a troubled glance. Two little turnips on legs. Did Roger give them enough to eat? Did he look after them properly? Their grandmother was probably exaggerating a bit. The air in the capital city alone was enough to sap the healthiest of creatures and gradually poison the hardiest. The girls may have had a few more bluish and obvious circles under their eyes than usual, but not many more. Roger didn't look too bad either.

He waited until midafternoon before talking to us about the team of journalists he had invited around for the following day. Judith and I looked at one another. Journalists.

Roger did not allow us to regain our breath. He explained to us that the worst thing that could happen was that silence should descend once again. That we needed to keep in the foreground and show that while tears continued to flow, at the same time, hope remained. We should trust him. The previous week, he had plastered the walls and *métro* stations with a photograph of Alice—taken three years earlier at a film festival in Sydney—and the caption GIVE HER BACK TO US. In the magazine *Elle* that week, she had shared a page with Paris Hilton—that pathetic blonde.

"You must stop," I told him. "Really. Don't stir up so much fuss for nothing."

He stared at me with a trace of contempt. "Have you lost hope then?"

"Not at all. But Roger, I don't see the point of all this."

"Give me one good reason not to do it. Tell me in what way this could harm her and I'll stop at once. I'm not like you, Francis. I can't just sit with my arms crossed and do nothing."

"You should go easy on the white stuff," I told him.

That evening, the weather was still good enough to cook a few spare ribs on the barbecue. The hiss of the surging tide could be heard in the distance; a dove was cooing in the neighbor's spruce tree, while its companion had just flown off toward the Rhune mountain, in the star-studded sky that floated calmly over the Pyrenees. He handed me some herbs.

His brow was knitted in an almost constant frown. But the moment he stopped frowning, he no longer looked so afflicted. Judith had not gone along with me in this analysis and had even reproached me for a certain hardness. Not just a certain hardness when I demanded tangible signs of his suffering—pallor, emaciation, sobbing . . . but also a certain foolishness in embarking on a path that led nowhere. "Would you be any further forward if he became ill? Would you feel mollified?"

In any case, his state of health did not alarm me. Could I

say that? Was I allowed to say that? Could I consider that he didn't look too bad, without being called a troublemaker?

"Let's go to the casino," I suggested to him when we had finished the meal. "Let's go and blow a bit of cash."

I got to my feet. I went upstairs to tell Judith and I stopped by the half-open door of the guest bedroom. Judith was reading something or other by Jane Austen to them. The twins had lumps in their throats and were snuggling up to their grandmother—who looked so young for her age that I felt choked once more. How could I have distanced myself from such a woman? I must be crazy, I would frequently tell myself. I should have been fulfilled to have married such a pretty brunette. A real one. I must be completely blind.

Johanna was also a brunette. Her full and magnificent head of hair had caught alight in a flash—as if flames were coming out of her head. I had clasped Alice to me but a few images had had time to imprint themselves on her mind, with the result that she had armies of shrinks on her tracks throughout all these years. The worries she had given me could have filled a stone quarry.

I loved Alice deeply, with all my heart, but I still felt a lingering resentment about everything she had made me put up with—a road accident, an overdose, a stay in a sobering-up cell, a drowning incident. This time, I was preparing myself to receive a fatal blow, and Judith could very well prove to be my only support during the unbearable ordeal that awaited me. I ought probably to keep the twins away in order to be close to her should everything disappear in a cloud of dust. I must not make a fool of myself.

When she looked at me, I smiled back and indicated that I was going out.

We walked along the beach. "I didn't think so," he said.

"Think what?"

"That you would sit around doing nothing."

"I have not sat around doing nothing."

"That's what I'm saying. That you haven't sat around doing nothing. I've said it, but I didn't think it."

The boards on which we were walking disappeared beneath the sand in places, then resurfaced looking as though they were covered in ashes. Seagulls circled overhead, hovering on the breeze. It was a cloudless night.

"What you have to understand," he said, "what you really have to understand, is that everything I do, I do for her."

"I should have preferred that you talked to us about it beforehand."

"Yes, I know. You've already told me. OK. I'm happy to spend the entire night apologizing if that's what you expect of me."

"It's a great idea. Go ahead."

"Listen, Francis, listen, it's not going to kill you. We mustn't *reduce* the search, we must *intensify* it. Intensify it, do you follow? That's the way these things work. The more they talk about her, the better it will be. What? You don't watch the news? You don't see what fate has in store for nonentities? You don't see that?"

I had a sudden longing to eat a waffle. The sea was like a vast, black, shiny screen teeming with blue filaments, over which streamed a wave of powerfully iodized air. From a beach hut where people were cooking came a good smell of vanilla-flavored pastry.

"I've never heard so much said about her," I said. "I see her everywhere. Even though she's not there. I think that's what I find so shocking. The contrast. To be honest with you."

"Fine. Very well. I can understand that it upsets you. But you must do it for her, Francis. Fucking hell, Francis."

I looked at him. In the half-light, his years spent getting stoned accentuated his haggard complexion, his mien of a crooked financier. I had told Alice my opinion of this young banker—the bank belonged to a branch of his family that had settled in Monaco—who spent entire days lying on the couch in his office in a state of delirium, his collar undone, canceling his appointments one by one, stoned out of his mind, etc. I had tried to open her eyes, but to no avail.

For my part, I married Judith. In these circumstances I could not object to marriage on formal grounds. In any case, I had not appeared firm enough, nor sufficiently convincing, and we had got married, within a month, at the church of Saint-Jean-Baptiste, when the cherry trees were in bloom, because fate had so decreed it, because we could no longer cope, because the flames had to be extinguished.

Those two years. Those following the accident. The nightmare years.

When I look at Roger today, and remind myself of the absolute zombie who married my daughter—and staggered up the aisle—I sometimes have to recognize that he managed very well, apart from the fact that he now dresses in Ralph Lauren from head to toe.

"There's a ransom demand, Francis," he told me, flinching as if I'd just stamped on his foot. I froze. "Sorry, but I wasn't allowed to talk about it," he added.

I cleared my throat. "She's alive?" I asked.

"What? Yeah . . . Sorry, yes . . . She's alive. But the police are stumbling on, of course."

"The ransom? What ransom? You talk to me about a ransom only now?"

I tossed half of my waffle in the garbage. My head spun for a few seconds and I decided to go and sit down on a nearby bench that abutted an old, hollowed-out tamarisk tree.

"You knew that I was fretting, that I feared the worst, you knew the anguish I was going through, but you had no mercy. You didn't think it right to afford me the slightest comfort, did you?"

He leaned toward me. "Hang on, Francis, hang on, let's be clear. I put Alice before everything else. I'm sorry. The police wanted to work in the greatest secrecy. I put Alice first. I told them: 'OK, go ahead, I've thought about it, I think you're right,' and I let them get on with it. I'm sorry."

I gazed at him for a moment. "But what are you on about?" I said to him. "How can you be so naïve . . . They bungled it, is that it? Is that what you're trying to tell me?"

Some seagulls were squabbling over my waffle—specks of white cream were flying around. In the shock of the moment, my hands were trembling.

Next morning, after an appalling night—Judith and I had made love dreadfully badly, following Roger's staggering revelation, and it had left me virtually impotent, something that was never good for our relationship the following day, or even in the days that followed, although she denied this—I was making my way toward the coffee machine when my son-in-law suddenly emerged to my right. It was seven o'clock in the morning, a time when it was unusual to see him up and about.

"The journalists are here," he said.

"What journalists?"

"You know very well, Francis. Don't play all innocent."

I suggested postponing the interview until the following day, but he immediately started to moan and weep, accusing me of ruining everything, of behaving like the worst and most selfish of people. "They've come specially from Paris. Didn't I tell you? Didn't I tell you how I've busted my ass getting them?"

The dawn was rising. I switched on the machine and made myself a Livanto, wondering what it was one needed to do in order to maintain the same sexual level, at my age, when you were going through what I was experiencing.

I stared at him. "You *simply* had to gather together the money, you *simply* had to follow their instructions, you *simply* had to bring them the dosh, that's all you had to do. Not try anything else. It *simply* needed a minimum of brains, Roger. You didn't have to play the smart guy, it wasn't complicated."

He deserved to suffer agonies for having put my daughter's fate in the hands of the police. Were I not convinced of the genuineness of his feelings for Alice, I think I could have hurled myself upon him. I could just hear him, the crazy idiot. Talking to other blithering idiots. Launching an operation with them. With this band of ghastly cowboys. This miserable band of ghastly cowboys who were incapable of paying a ransom without making a mess of everything. "If I didn't feel so awful, I'd burst out laughing," I told him. "So much stupidity leaves one bewildered. Honestly, Roger."

He was hopping from one foot to the other, his head lowered, groaning quietly to himself, in a hurry that we should move on. Above the sea, the sky was cloudless and bright. Young men were on their way down to the beach from the parking lots, walking a little stiffly, with their boards under their arms. In the town, the café owners were setting up their tables, and at the delicatessen they were putting out their hams. The market was about to open. The first plane for Paris had taken off and was flying in a steep curve over the bay.

"We're at a deadlock," he said to me plaintively.

I said nothing, I had understood him. "A complete deadlock," he muttered.

According to him, my taking part in the interview was crucial. The trembling in my hands had not completely gone away. I called A.-M. I had spoken to her the day before and informed her that she had been right, that it had been a kidnapping. "But we didn't speak about the press," I said to her. "And right now, I've got Roger with me, who's talking to me about a meeting with some journalists, about an interview arranged with them . . . yes, I've told him . . . that he should stop now, I've told him . . . He's nodding to say yes, he's understood . . . no further initiatives, yes, I think he's understood, he's nodding that he has."

Had I, for my part, actually taken in that the interview was to be filmed? He had a knack for annoying me. He swore that he had told me, but I had no memory of it. He maintained that it was too late to cancel the meeting. He had not been running, but he suddenly seemed out of breath. I ought to ponder, according to him. I ought to ponder long and hard. Never stop thinking about my daughter. Do everything. Put aside all misplaced pride. Swallow all pride.

Ride roughshod over all pride if necessary. Be on the eight o'clock news.

That was the last straw. Roger was perspiring, but he wouldn't budge. *Paris-Match* had offered to publish the interview in the next issue and *Voici* was rummaging around in its archives again—after the telephone calls Roger had made to them.

According to him, I should open my eyes. I should observe what was going on. If you began with the principle that it was better to be famous than to be anonymous, I had no right to hesitate. I should go out in front of the cameras and beg the kidnappers to let her live, make them another offer. I should tell them what a wonderful girl she was, what an exceptional mother she was, what a delightful creature they were holding—not to mention the César award she had carried off six years ago, the promise of her young career, her campaign against AIDS, etc. "Do I have the right to dissolve into tears?" I asked.

He sent Judith to explain to me that we had to make the most of the ransom demand in order to sustain people's feelings about Alice. Because I had sold a few hundred thousand books, I was not entirely unknown, and he was only too well aware of the impact my moaning would have on the small screen. "I'm aware of it too, Roger. It's extremely embarrassing. I don't think it will help our cause."

So had I made up my mind to wait until they sent me one of her ears through the post? Or did these things only happen to other people, by my reckoning?

They set up the lighting in the drawing room. They thought that I had a problem with my eyes—which was suddenly blown up out of all proportion. A girl made us stand up. They put the microphones on us.

My insides froze.

"We're ready when you are, sir. Are you cold?"

One of us, at least, appeared satisfied. At one point in the evening, Roger put his hand on my shoulder and said that Alice had the father she deserved. I had been perfect.

A moment earlier, I had caught Judith in the middle of a telephone conversation she was having, speaking in a low voice, in Spanish; I don't speak Spanish. I had stepped back into the shadows in silence; it seemed to me that she had been speaking lovingly in the half light.

I had not been an ideal husband for Johanna, and I was not a better one for Judith, it appeared. There were probably lessons to have been drawn that I had failed to draw.

"I know what you're thinking," Roger said to me. I looked up at him. "But it was necessary," he went on. "Trust me, for once."

I turned around. Judith had come into the room for a moment to tell us that she had to go back to the office—it was eleven o'clock at night. I did no more than nod my head and gaze after her. I found it almost insulting that she had not found a better excuse. That she had not taken the trouble. Going back to the office at eleven o'clock at night. It was so implausible.

I wondered whether I should not go and talk about it with A.-M., whether I should not arrange to have her followed so that I could know the truth.

"I'd prefer us not to complicate matters," she said to me. "I'm in the middle of examining this ransom business. I'd like to concentrate on that."

"Very well," I replied. "Very well, I won't dwell on it."

"If we want to stay on good terms, Francis. Believe me. Consult someone else about your wife."

Without reflecting on the matter, I immediately thought of Jérémie. I dangled a few banknotes at him to carry out an easy job: I simply wanted to know how Judith spent her time, to know where she went, whom she saw. "Five hundred now, and five hundred at the end of the week. I'll pay for the cost of sandwiches and gas. Is it yes? Then you're on, old friend. But there's no point telling your mother about our arrangement. I don't want any problems with her."

Judith came home at about one o'clock in the morning. I got up to look through the keyhole. I watched her undress. I noticed her calm and collected manner.

The following morning, Roger shoved half a dozen newspapers in front of me and declared that we had done good work. He showed me the picture of Alice on the Yahoo! home page and some bits of the video in which I had found the means to shed a tear, which they had zoomed in on.

A.-M. had gone up to Paris in order to discover more about the failed ransom operation. "She may surprise us," I said. "She's a tough one. I get on well with her. And the advantage she has, the enormous advantage she has, is her availability. She's not trying to look after fifty thousand things at the same time. Unlike the police. With A.-M. everything will be gone through with a fine-tooth comb. She's a meticulous woman. I trust her. Good God, Roger, discovering fresh hope is an amazing thing. I had lost it completely, of course, but . . . and here I am breathing more easily. You can't imagine. At least I know that she's not lying at the bottom of a lake. At least I know that she's not at the bottom of a crevice. Of course I'm still worried. Naturally. You and I know that there are crazy people everywhere. I'm dead frightened. I'm dead frightened. Why are they taking so long to get in touch with us? Why are they spinning things out? What's the point? But I prefer that, Roger, I prefer that to deafening silence. Which was destroying me. As you must have been only too aware. All that time without any news, Roger. I spent all that time without any news."

Yet I did not mean to give him too hard a time. I could see that he was giving his all—even if I was not sure whether his strategy was the right one or whether it had little point, or whether it was even appropriate. In a certain way, he was now part of the family. And this family was so decimated that it would have seemed very unwise to get rid of the least member of it, to chop off the slightest head. Even if it belonged to an ex-junkie turned banker.

I had known Roger for ten years or more now, and although he had caused me a few serious worries during the early months of their marriage—every month had to be reckoned with, every month brought its share of problems and anxieties, every month hung in the balance—I was obliged to admit, yet again, that he had displayed a certain strength of character in pulling through. He really did. In fact, Roger was the perfect example of the type who had kicked the habit with a flourish. From the day Alice became pregnant. He had sworn that he would give up hard drugs and throw them all down the lavatory. I could testify to the fact. He wanted me to be present at the scene. To be there to hear his pledge.

When I recalled that time, my jaw clenched.

"The mechanism was triggered too early," he eventually explained to me. "I don't know how it is operated, but when the suitcase is opened, why, the thing works somehow or other, and it sends a good spray of indelible ink all over the banknotes, as well as the guy's head, and it functions perfectly, most of the time."

"My grandfather died at Verdun because his rifle, his 1886 Lebel, jammed during the attack."

"The inspector saw the suitcase explode on his lap.

Wham! For no reason. In the great hall of the Gare de Lyon. He was ten minutes early for the meeting. There's still a blue stain on the ground."

In my case, feeling hopeful again made me feel strangely nauseous. And so I walked to the sea while Roger gave his daughters something to eat. And just as well I did, because a spasm made me bend double just as I was setting foot in the water.

Vomiting in the sea provides a few benefits. For a moment I was reeling like a drunkard, then I moved a few feet away and bent forward to wash my face. Fortunately, it was no longer the height of summer, with all the crowds, and the nearest passersby looked like matchsticks. The dog that was with them came bounding toward me at full speed, plunged into the water in a single leap, and began to feed eagerly on the floating matter; in the meantime his master trotted up, yelling: "Rex! Rex!"

I didn't have the stamina of the old days, and I was growing more fragile. More sentimental, let us say the word. Alice's absence brought back the ghosts of her mother and her sister, and I didn't need that. And now, *hope.*

An absurd hope, one that depended on nothing very tangible, that gave you a pain in the guts, that sent threads of mucus flying into the breeze.

The image of the car ablaze came back to me—my Saab 900 convertible, with its leather interior, which I never left outside at night. That unbelievable sight. The roaring of the flames. Alice's face buried in my chest. Her cries, her shuddering. While I watched the two women burn like torches, their arms like the branches of a chandelier. Johanna, their mother. Olga, the elder of our two daughters.

I didn't need any further ordeal.

Neither did I need Judith and me to be more or less involved in a process of breaking up. At the same time.

Where does that feeling one sometimes gets that life is mocking you come from?

My books were selling fairly well at the time and, on the day of the accident, we were on our way to Pamplona, all four of us. I had just sold a story (for a high price) to the German edition of *Playboy,* but Johanna and I had had one hell of an argument the previous day and nobody had uttered a word since we left the house.

I was waiting for the moment when the blows would come raining down on my head. I kept my eyes glued to the road and held the steering wheel with both hands. It seemed to me that certain things had a surface, of course, but no depth, and so they ought not to be given more importance than they deserved; Johanna, and it was unfortunate, did not share this sort of opinion.

It was to do with a fairly ordinary literary festival in the Swiss canton of Grisons. The readings followed on from one another until daybreak and you could drink as much as you wanted. In Grisons. On the edge of the inhabited world, in other words. Marlène and I had laughed on the day of our arrival when we discovered they had booked us into a double room. Outside, you could hear the sound of cattle, of bells, the clatter of wooden shoes. It was almost an hour's journey from the station on the post office bus, along a tiny road that ran along precipices. As soon as it grew dark, large quantities of absinthe began to be passed around and each reading session generated such powerful surges of adrenaline that it was hard to restrain oneself. Lost in the depths of Grisons, a stone's throw from Sils-Maria, where Nietzsche liked to roam. Lord Jesus. But none of this managed to engage Johanna's clemency.

I was very keen on Hemingway at that time and the idea of a trip to Pamplona delighted me. But even though the morning was bright and clear, the air soft, and the motorway empty, my illusions were quickly shattered.

I had grabbed my phone and changed publishers straightaway, but that was not enough. Johanna felt hurt. The crisis lasted for two days. Didn't sleep the first night; in fits and starts the following one. I reckoned that the holidays and a few gory bullfights would change our ideas. They had to. The atmosphere was dreadful.

I turned off on an exit ramp and parked alongside the cafeteria, in a bit of shade. I looked questioningly at Johanna. Not obtaining any response, I got out. I was wondering what expression Ernesto would have used had he been me. Then Alice got out, too. I was wondering what expression the girls would make should Johanna explain to them why she loathed my guts. I was frightened that their powers of judgment might not be fully developed yet and that they might blame me a little too readily. Having said that, I did not delude myself about the reprieve I was being given. I knew that Johanna would eventually give in. She had told me so. She made no secret of it.

Alice caught up with me outside the shop. I waited for her as I gazed at the blue sky above the forests that surrounded us. As he crossed the Pyrenees, Hemingway had filled his lungs with the air of these verdant, mossy mountains. The saintly man.

After this, Alice and I would live together for two years. Two terrible years. In a three-room apartment. When it should have been twice the size. Or even three times.

I was in no mood to read to the girls. I told Roger that I hoped he would understand. To appear more convincing, I pretended that I needed to think about a possible future novel and I left him to look after his offspring while I withdrew to the bottom of the garden adopting a look of inspiration.

Jérémie appeared as soon as Roger had gone inside. I noticed he had a notebook in his hand.

"I think you're mistaken," he said to me. "She spent the day taking people to houses. I have the list."

"I'd like to be mistaken. Let me see this list, hmm? But

tell me. Do you know anyone who enjoys throwing his money away? Do you take me for an idiot? . . . Continue to watch her. Do as I tell you. Keep your eyes peeled. She's an intelligent woman, you know."

Of course he took me for an idiot—I was personally convinced that she was pulling the wool over his eyes. I pointed to the fridge, in case he should want anything. He shook his head. He did not understand that it was possible to let a woman like that slip through your hands, were you lucky enough to have one.

"Go and get yourself a nice goat's-milk ice cream," I persisted. "Don't be shy."

One could be shy and hold up a service station with a hunting rifle simultaneously. Here was the proof.

Roger, who had come across him once or twice, found him disturbing, and his mother had been begging him to find a job quickly ever since he had come out of prison, reckoning that idleness was the worst state of mind in which to find oneself.

I gazed after him as he walked away, his dog at his heels. "When are you going to decide to give him a name?" I called out.

When Judith returned from the agency, she asked me why I looked so pale. Very indicative of the amount of interest she took in me, I reckoned.

◆

Same thing the following day. She had quietly sold her houses. And the same thing the day after. "Listen, I don't think I'm going to be able to do that much longer," he told me.

"Do what, Jérémie? You're not going to be able to do *what* much longer?"

"Follow her. I don't like it much."

"Oh, for pity's sake. Don't be so pathetic." I placed my hands on his shoulders. "It's a personal favor I'm asking you, Jérémie." I looked him straight in the eyes. "It's not the right moment to let me down."

"Listen, I don't really like spying on people."

"Of course not. Thank goodness. It's just for this once. Put yourself in my shoes for a second. I need someone whom I can trust."

Apart from me, I didn't know what other company he kept. "Do you want us to discuss your fee again?"

He said it was all right. He added that I would probably come to the conclusion that my wife had no lover. "Until there's proof to the contrary," I said, "I agree."

He leaned toward me.

"But what difference can it make to you, after all? What good will it do you? I thought you weren't getting on together."

"I want to know the truth. That's all, I would see to it myself were not Alice occupying my entire thoughts at the moment. Believe me . . . You need a job, don't forget . . . It's always better to have a bit of money in your pockets. Hold on for a week or two. Think about it for a moment, old friend. Remember that people are washing windows on the sixtieth floor of buildings for barely one thousand euros a month."

I was probably wrong to bring up this aspect of the situation with a boy who had chosen a murky path. I was probably wrong to tell a young man that jobs existed for less than one thousand euros. That very morning, I had seen a man walking along a crane shaft, in the wind, miles above the ground. I hoped he had fastened his helmet—a yellow helmet that was a target for the first rays of the sun.

"You would have the best teacher imaginable," I told him. "That's not to be sniffed at."

"I know. That's not the problem."

"Stop. Please. Good grief. Look around you. Jérémie. Look around you. It's not a joking matter, you know. Short of trying to scour every service station in the country, I don't get the feeling it's such a bad option, being a detective. I wouldn't have minded, on reflection. Following people. Mind you, it's rather what I do when I write. It wouldn't have altered me very much. Let's be clear: nothing's going to force you to do that all your life. Get yourself back in the saddle, and I'm sure that afterward everything will turn out fine. A private detective, eh? It's better than being a croupier, in any case."

This type of conversation made him walk faster, then he overtook me and set off at a trot with his dog. Yet again. There was nothing that could be done. At the end of the day, A.-M. was probably right to be worried. Six years in prison was not a trivial matter. The pain ran deep. The pain had deep roots.

On the other end of the line, A.-M. said it was extremely kind of me to discuss this matter with him. "It's only natural," I replied. "If it can help you, that's great."

Something was bothering her. It was still too soon to talk about it, but she would keep me informed. I didn't have the energy to try to find out more. "Is everything OK in Paris? D'you get time to enjoy yourself a bit?" I knew that she was seeing a woman in the Les Halles district. "Sort of," she answered. "You know how it is. You really have to be on your toes to establish a long-lasting relationship."

I had had the opportunity to see a photo of her girlfriend. She had the look of a schoolteacher.

"I reckon this dog is doing him a lot of good," I said. "I reckon this dog is your best ally. I only wish he'd get a name, don't you agree?"

You only had to look at them together: the abandoned dog and the young lad who had left prison—it was a poem in itself.

"But you're right to be very careful," I continued.

"I'm *extremely* careful in that respect."

"I believe it would be the wrong moment."

I didn't know her sufficiently well to gauge from her

reaction whether he had uncovered the truth. Something told me that it wasn't something he'd especially appreciate.

"His father was the most pathetic sexual partner imaginable," she said in a hollow voice.

"You certainly did the right thing. I don't doubt it for a moment. But one has to be wary of a boy's image of his father. Touching upon it is like handling dynamite. It's best to know, you see. Don't we spend our lives making up for the mistakes and humiliations of our fathers?"

When I put down the phone, Judith was sitting opposite me. She had come back from her jogging, exhaling a mist of invisible particles around her.

"Is everything all right?" she asked me.

"What are you talking about? Some things are fine, others less so."

She gave a slight sigh, then looked up as if to indicate that she did not want to get involved in these matters. "Nothing new?" I shook my head.

"I trust her entirely. If there's anything to find, she will find it."

We used to call Alice *our* daughter, but Alice was not her daughter, there was no question about that. I had all the proof I wanted in the coolness with which she dealt with this situation when I knew that Johanna would have been worried stiff, just as I, her father, was totally drained.

Knowing beforehand the gist of the remarks she would make if I were to blame her for her lack of empathy, I was careful not to say anything critical in this respect. What good would it do? Our most memorable rows, in the past, had blown up in connection with Alice—up until the day we decided that the subject was closed.

"I've nothing against your friend," she said after staring at me for a moment. "I'd just like to be sure that you have made the right choice."

"I've known this woman since we sat on school benches together. We used to go to anti–Vietnam War demonstrations. Whom I could trust more?"

"Did you sleep with her?"

"How do you expect me to know? Our evenings were somewhat hazy in those days. There were lots of substances going around. In any case, I wouldn't say she's a girlfriend."

I examined her legs and her arms closely, but discreetly, for any signs or marks, but I found nothing convincing.

I tried to obtain her favors once more, just to see. After the fiasco of the other night, I wanted to find out the truth. And so, when it was dark, without further ado, I flicked a comb through my hair and let myself into her bedroom.

She had switched off the light. A glimmer of light shone through the thick curtains. I drew near. It was as if she was expecting me. The sheets had been thrown back. She was wearing her white Petit Bateau underwear.

In actual fact—I quickly realized—she was asleep. Or pretending to sleep. The weather was mild, we had not yet turned on the heating. In passing, by the way, it had seemed sensible to go and live in the South when we saw the way things were going: the bill from the energy company, for example—better to spend the winter using one log rather than having to burn a whole stack of timber. The Basque Country was one of the right solutions. The countryside was beautiful, the grass was green, the cattle were the same as those in Switzerland. There were places where you could fish for rainbow trout in the shade of wonderful undergrowth—as long as you had prepared the flies correctly—while beyond stretched the open sea with its host of nubile girls surfing in their Eres bathing suits. Some might prefer Corsica. Or a few villages on the Côte d'Azur, but that was really all. The shores of Lake Garda, at a pinch. There weren't many such places.

Wake her? Should I wake her? And risk passing for some sort of beast?

Without being certain that I wouldn't start to droop along the way?

Besides, I wasn't turned on yet. I looked outside, holding the curtain open with one finger. The dunes were deserted. In the distance, the lights of the casino fluttered in the tamarisk trees. I thought of Alice once more. I noticed that the windowsill was flaking.

I turned around and placed my prick on the pillow, close to Judith's face. I used to love being sucked off, and, by behaving like this, I hoped to arouse my erection, but nothing happened. And yet I was an inch away from her lips, from her still astonishingly voluptuous lips, though, to my great consternation, this did not mean that blood went rushing to swell my loins. I withdrew immediately. All I needed would be for her to find me in this unfortunate position, in the role of the impotent lecher. I shuddered at the thought of it. I stepped back a few feet. "You've got Viagra coming to you, old man," I told myself. "OK, I think we're getting there. That's it. Let's go for it . . ." I was reeling.

Back in my bedroom, I was sweating, panting. Frozen.

A few days later, Jérémie's dog was smashed against the rocks by one of those enormous waves that had been rolling in all afternoon—there had been a change in the moon. The dog's skeleton had been battered to pieces and its head reduced to a pulp.

Two other dogs were found, some cats, and a few cattle washed down from the Adour River—as happens after every big storm—carrying with it drugs, wads of cash, cigarette cartons, etc. The town hall employed men to clean away these more or less inappropriate objects, some of them bloodstained, from the beach. Jérémie's dog hadn't a single tooth left, and its tongue had been severed.

Dusk was falling. I knew he was searching for his dog. A few hours earlier, he had arrived, slightly concerned, to ask me if I had seen it—occasionally the dog went for a walk with the girls. I had tried to calm him, reminding him just how quick, intelligent, and alert the animal had shown itself to be—even to my eyes, someone who is not very interested in domestic pets—and therefore clever enough to take shelter if the weather was turning for the worse. His complexion was almost gray. Behind him, the sea was roaring, low clouds were streaming past like submarines in the bronze sky. "Keep me posted," I'd said to him. "Use your phone. Have faith."

A moment later, the storm had broken, and during the two hours that followed I completely forgot about him and his dog.

Roger had set off to do goodness knows what in town, and the two little girls, who claimed they had seen a flash of lightning pass through the house, were clinging to me and trembling like leaves, while the sky was lit up and deafening explosions shook the entire house.

They were tugging at my sweater. I had one of them on each knee. They were bending forward to yell into my ear when the heavens unleashed a flash of lightning right over the dunes. A sudden apparition, in the garden, just as the storm was moving away, was the cause of their latest cries: a sort of motionless specter on his milky-white, steaming shoulders, from which huge drops trickled.

Jérémie was holding the remains of his dog in his arms.

"Listen, girls," I said. "You must go up to your bedroom."

But they had already jumped up, had opened the bay

window, and were rushing over to Jérémie before I was able to step in. They were drenched from head to foot in a trice.

I ushered everyone into the kitchen. The girls were weeping noisily and were throwing tantrums. Jérémie appeared to be in a state of shock. I took the animal from him and went to lay it on top of the dryer. A stuffed doll, weighing ten kilos or so, scarcely recognizable, and unpleasant to touch.

I made everyone get out of the kitchen. The twins were clinging to me and sobbing, convinced that I could do something to bring this dog back to life. I dragged them over to the bar so that I could pour a dram of 70° whisky—o river of fire, o reviving force—for someone who seemed to be desperately in need of it.

"Let's sit down," I said. "Let's try to control our breathing. OK, girls? Calm down. And you, Jérémie, drain that glass, please. I'm going to get you another. There's no point in howling, you know. Where's your father? I'd like to know where he is. You're soaked. Go and find some towels. Jérémie and I will dry you. Won't we, Jérémie? Won't we, Jérémie? My poor old friend. What a wretched business, by the way. The poor dog. But come along, sit down, don't just stand there like an idiot. Yes, do, don't worry about that. It's waterproof leather. Don't bother about that. Try to relax. Breathe in. Breathe in deeply. So you found him like that, on the rocks? Beneath the lighthouse, you say? Do you think he fell from up there? That he bumped into a couple of irritable gays going at it in the bushes? Hmm. Maybe. It's not impossible. I know they don't like being disturbed. But I don't imagine you've any proof of what you're suggesting. These guys must have chucked your dog in the water? And why would they do that, Jérémie? Look at me. What's the matter? Wait a second. Listen to me, girls. I'm not joking anymore."

While they set off in the direction of the airing cupboard upstairs, I leaned over toward him:

"You went to bug them, is that it? Don't tell me you did that, Jérémie. Look at me. Did you go to bug these guys? But what on earth got into your head? You see the result? Your father didn't help you, as far as that's concerned. I'm telling you frankly, he did you no favors."

His head dropped so low that I could no longer see his face. I didn't know whether water was dripping from him or whether he was crying. A smell of damp dog now pervaded the house. A small puddle was forming at his feet. One more appalling story. A story of total wastefulness—for which the dog paid the price.

"Listen to me. We can't bury a dog in the forest in weather like this, absolutely not. That would be verging on madness, do you hear? Digging a grave in weather like this, you must be joking. Using the headlights, I suppose? In twenty inches of mud. In teeming rain." They pointed out that the storm had died down. That the moon had dried the darkened fields as it rose.

I helped him carry the dog to the trunk of my car while

the girls searched the house, gathering up all the flashlights they could find; I could hear the cutlery flying around in the drawers, the cupboard doors slamming.

As I went out, I had the feeling that I was diving into a pool of warm water. I left a message for Judith informing her of the predicament we had got into, were she to come home and find the house empty. If she ever did come home. Something I was never entirely sure about. "I don't even know where you are," I added in a tone of voice that struck me as plaintive.

As time went by, I was becoming increasingly sentimental. If I went on like this, I would soon become ridiculous.

Half an hour later, we pulled up in the middle of the forest. It was still raining quite hard. It was still dark. In the back, the little girls were still spluttering into their handkerchiefs. I turned round to them and made them promise not to move from there while Jérémie and I were working.

Very quickly, our task became a quagmire.

The earth was dark and thick. As we dug deeper, the hole filled with water. Through the misted-up windows of the car, the two girls were watching us open-eyed. The rain, all around us, was spitting like bacon in a frying pan. "I'm not going to go on asking you the same question until the end of time," I said, almost yelling so that he should hear me. "Don't count on it. So, one last time, I'm asking you, Jérémie, *are you all right*? . . . If not I'll drive you to the emergency room right away to be looked after, OK? I recommend you find your tongue again quickly, OK?"

To begin with, he nodded. I told him that wouldn't be enough.

"Yeah, it's OK," he muttered finally. "I don't want to talk."

These types of windbreakers with hoods that we had brought with us, very fashionable with campers and tourists, were sticking to our skins the way transparent plastic film clings to vacuum-packed food.

"They murdered my dog!" he grunted between his teeth before beginning to dig frantically again.

I looked at him for a moment. "I can't get over the fact that you could have done that," I said to him eventually. "I'm flabbergasted. Your mother really will be pleased. I think she'll be really proud of you. Doubly so. But for a start, you don't know a thing. You accuse these people, but you don't know a thing. You've no right to do that."

He stood up and looked at me fiercely, but no word came from his lips. He suddenly hurled his shovel to the ground and set off furiously to collect his dog.

We had already talked about this, he knew what I thought and what my views were on the subject. Nevertheless, I had admitted that when it had to do with the father or the mother, it did not make things any easier for the child. I could understand his confusion. I could understand that things weren't quite right inside this child's head—and yet it wasn't as if we were having to be protected from rabies or poliomyelitis or dyscalculia.

He stood still for a moment, in front of the open trunk of

the car, while torrential rain beat down on his head, before bending down to pick up his dog. Once again, I was happy to admit that the loss was tough for a young fellow who had just come out after six years in prison. In any case, all this was not very good for my coachwork; I didn't know whether Audi treated the inside of the trunk with antirust.

The following day, we were obliged to go back to put up a cross or risk dealing with a double nervous breakdown— Alice had brought them up very badly—and being labeled an infidel; Alice had managed to have them baptized and religion was already seeping into their young and hazy minds. Since when had people not been putting crosses on graves? What sort of a grandfather did they have after all?

The weather was fine after the previous night's storms. The sky was a washed-out blue. Imagining that we might use the opportunity to find a few cèpe mushrooms, I agreed—on condition that they didn't expect me to be involved with preparing the thing, for I wasn't in the mood for that.

I was unsure whether to wake their father. I was having breakfast. I took a look at my mail. Since I was still writing a few stories for newspapers and had become unusually obsessive about proof corrections—I was well known for being the worst in the whole country, the kind who really did split hairs—I was still fairly busy, and this meant I could not devote my time to their games, their ceremonies, their fussy demands, and I had therefore left them in the garage, asking them to be careful not to injure themselves with any sharp tool or other.

As for me, I could no more bring myself to put two bits of wood together—or anything else—as long as there was a chance that Alice was still alive.

Judith had returned in the middle of the night. For the time being, she was asleep.

What was the point of waking her up either? On reflection, talking to the twins was what probably suited me best on this dazzlingly bright day. A light breeze was coming from the sea, mingled with the scent of tamarisks. I found the girls and examined the cross they had made with bits of wood from a crate and bent nails. "Good work," I said to them in a friendly way as I operated the garage door. "I know someone who's going to be pleased."

I wasn't talking about Jérémie. However, it was he whom I spotted in my rearview mirror when I switched on the engine. I gave a frosty glance at the girls. Then I reversed and stopped alongside him.

"I'll tell you what I think," I said after contemplating him for a moment. "Go back home. Let us deal with this."

It was as if he were clenching his teeth with all his might. In the end, I asked him to get in. "I was saying that for your own good," I said as I drove off. From a canvas bag he carried on his shoulder, he took out a cross that had been astonishingly and elaborately carved and polished, and that gleamed like a fine, old wooden floor that had been newly polished.

The girls cried out in delight. He shrugged his shoulders. He explained that he had developed this pastime in prison. That this carefully decorated cross was the least he owed his friend, his companion.

It was so childish. On a level with the twins, who would soon be asking for holy water; yet the girls were still at an age to bury dead beetles . . . and he at an age to hold up a service station.

He must have spent the entire night there. It was so childish. I didn't need to see the state his hands were in to imagine the ordeal he was going through, but I found it somewhat hard to sympathize, considering what I was going through myself.

In any case, his presence had a negative effect on all of us. I suspected that he was taking advantage of his mother's absence in order not to eat anything. Before she left, A.-M. had filled the freezer with individual portions that could be put straight into the microwave, but this seemed to require an effort he could not manage. He was growing extremely pale.

He didn't utter a word throughout the journey. I didn't know whether I was right or wrong to go through this foolish procedure with them. And yet it was from me, I supposed, being the eldest in the group, that one might have expected a little good sense. To have put a stop right away to this jaunt, which did not show any of us in a good light.

However, I had not done this. I had not clapped my hands to bring the three of them down to earth. I had not put my foot down. I had opened the car door and asked Jérémie to get in.

I would have found it very difficult to say what it was I was giving in to, but the result was here, on this road that meandered through the brush and climbed up toward the hill, in an atmosphere that was as sultry as one could imagine.

The cross that Jérémie had carved and the skill and passion that he had obviously devoted to its construction made the process even more solemn, even more unbearable. Just what one needed to avoid. But it was too late to turn back now.

A little while later, Jérémie was looking at my CD player and scrolling through my lists. "Can I put on Current 93?" he asked as we were nearing our objective; a shower of golden petals that had fallen from the trees rustled on the road, still shimmering after the strong intermittent downpours during the night. I gave in. What did it matter? I could see the twins in the rearview mirror. I could see their hands joined, I could see their lips moving, and I wondered whether they were reciting some sort of prayer.

We had buried the dog in the teeming rain but we were now dealing with the funeral ceremony on one of those infinitely graceful autumn days for which we were the envy of the entire world. The bay that stretched out behind us, from the Spanish coast to the horizon, was like a casket of jewels that sparkled with amethysts, sapphires, turquoises, etc. Ernesto often used to walk here. I mean to say that Ernest Hemingway often used to walk here. He always said that there was no better place in the world for a writer. He was hardly exaggerating. He used to come to these parts regularly, accompanied by one of my aunts, to pick cèpes and take a siesta beneath the ancient oak and chestnut trees. That stout fellow.

Jérémie had brought along a hammer and some nails the size of a finger to put up the two crosses. The tree trunk beneath which his dog was buried seemed as hard as stone. He had asked me to leave the doors open so that we could hear some of those dismal songs that David Tibet specialized in; meanwhile the grim hammer blows echoed through the forest and the twins squelched about in the mud searching for leaves and flowers as decorations. I stood back a little, chewing on nicotine gum, pretending not to notice the flight of the crows directly above the clearing where the scene was taking place. I was longing to wander about in the brush, for I could detect a very distinct smell of fresh mushrooms. Alice adored cèpes. Tears began to streak down my cheeks, just thinking about this. As I drove off along the wrong road, I could sense Jérémie's silent approval.

I spent a good part of the afternoon in the garden, cleaning the basket I had used to collect the cèpes in the forest and wondering about Jérémie, about what would become of him.

Roger had taken his daughters to the cinema after criticizing me for being a second-rate grandfather; he was referring to the state in which I had brought them back, red-eyed and covered in mud from head to foot, etc. I had not reacted. I needed a little calm after the business of the burial.

When we got back, Judith had already gone out. I called her, then found her bedroom empty, her bed unmade. I rang Jérémie's number to ask him to start his tailing job straightaway, but there was no answer. Shit! What was he doing with his telephone? At this time of day, she may have been in a hotel bedroom, with her lover. We had to make sure. But Jérémie was not answering.

Roger and the girls had left for the 4:30 showing. The sky was beginning to turn pink. Judith's hours were becoming more and more unreasonable. I was confident. I knew that, sooner or later, she would make a mistake and would be caught. So long as Jérémie kept his eyes open and didn't just sit sprawled in an armchair waiting for the world to end.

Before reaching his voice mail, one had to endure forty-five seconds listening to a particularly agitated English group who nearly burst one's eardrums. "OK, Jérémie. Call me back. Urgently. As soon as you get this message. Call me extremely urgently, will you?" But evening came and he did not ring back.

Judith could take all the time she wanted with an amateur like this on her tracks. I carried my mushrooms into the kitchen, rinsed them, and then went back outside. I called Jérémie again. "Listen to me. I need to know if you've got any eggs. Whether you can let me have some or whether I have to go down to the town. So, please, pick up your phone. The girls will be back and they'll be starving. There'll be a scene. Will you please get back to me? Thank you."

I had probably asked for it—I'd been unable, at least, to prevent myself wanting a double, a duplicate of Johanna and nothing else—I had probably deserved what was happening to me as far as that was concerned. There was no going back on that. God knows, I hadn't wanted any of this. All I wanted at the moment was to be able to take my punishment and get away without it causing too much damage. I knew all the facts. In her place, I would certainly have done the same as Judith. Or worse, who knows?

Be that as it may, I rang Jérémie again. We had agreed that I could contact him at any time in view of the task that I had entrusted him with. I reminded him of this curtly, via his answering machine, not forgetting to thank him for the eggs.

The more time went by, the more convinced I became that Judith was giving herself to another man in a nearby bedroom. The region swarmed with those small, luxurious inns, offering half board, that were perfectly discreet and real havens; if one wanted to abduct a woman and win her over, well, this area was hard to beat.

Such a scenario set my teeth on edge. I felt unable to keep still. I stood up to cut the cèpes into strips and slices, and felt short of breath. I felt deeply ashamed as I noted my pathetic reaction, my futile restlessness, and I could feel my cheeks flushing. Yet a good part of me persisted in feeling this way.

Such visions, such horrors came into my mind that I almost suffocated. I could almost hear her moans, the words she whispered into the man's ear as she perspired on top of him. Impossible to escape from them. Clutching a dish towel, I sat down.

Night was beginning to fall, bringing with it cooler air that was extremely welcome for my temples were burning. I stood up. I opened the butane gas canister and lit the grill.

I browned the cèpes. I chopped the garlic and the parsley. As I got older, I thought I had grown out of these things. I thought I had understood that they were not worth the trouble one used to take over them, I thought I had realized that one had attained a higher level, that one no longer had to play these foolish games, that one could be rid of them, and yet here I was shivering in the twilight like a schoolboy, totally ill equipped, shattered.

But what on earth was this idiot Jérémie doing then? I was beginning to have had enough. I was overwhelmed by what I was visualizing, overwhelmed by the way she had surrendered herself into the arms of the chimpanzee who had her in all sorts of positions. I chewed another piece of nicotine gum; sometimes I had nightmares in which I had run short of it and was planning to go and break into a drugstore with a hammer.

I finished the cooking and then slid the mushrooms onto a plate that I then covered. As an omelet, it was one of the best dishes in the world. In fact, I was never surprised when I heard tell that this or that person had succumbed to the charm of this region; some extremely well-known writers used to travel down from Paris to investigate our way of life and to take notes, and these guys had intuition.

I got into my car. In less than three minutes, after champing at the bit among the pine trees and the heather, I parked purposefully opposite the house in which he lived with his mother and got ready to teach him his job—which consisted in not falling asleep while the client's wife was committing adultery.

I persuaded myself that I would explain to him that he ought to take his work much more seriously if he intended to make a name for himself in the profession; that he couldn't allow his own moods to distract him from his task. In any way. Not in these grim times when holding your head above water required all your efforts, when keeping yourself and your family alive did not come easily. Was there anyone who still doubted that market forces would have no mercy on those who did not heed them? Could anyone still claim that the Western world was making positive progress?

The moon was shining. I remained at the wheel for a

second, hoping that a rush of pride might make me turn back, but nothing of the kind occurred.

Judith was choosing the worst moment to do this to me. I was therefore doubly angry with her and I had no difficulty getting out of my car, walking through the Lémos' little garden that consisted largely of tufts of grass and sand, adorned with a few pinecones that had rolled there, as well as some cream-colored pine needles, and knocking at the door. There was a light shining on the first floor. I rang the bell. "Jérémie, it's me!" I shouted, hopping from one foot to the other.

I waited a short while, then I tried the door handle. It was open. I could hear the muffled sounds of Joy Division, which he was still playing. The kitchen light was on. "Would you have some eggs you could lend me?" I called out, making my way toward the fridge. "I rang, but you didn't answer." Radio silence.

I came across a slice of green ham, a bit of black Basque pâté, some yellow spaghetti, very yellow, very stiff, almost translucent. Two solitary eggs, laid in the last century, were squabbling in a corner, alongside a chunk of half-decayed goat cheese. A.-M. wondered whether her son ate properly when she was away. I would not be able to reassure her for the time being.

You could not count the anxieties that Jérémie caused on the fingers of one hand. All the more reason, I told myself, to look after him and to pack him off right away on the track of my wife, who was probably dining by candlelight at this very moment, in a sweet, modest country bedroom, dressed simply in a minuscule nightdress no thicker than a micron, with her hair awry, etc., her cheeks flushed.

The living room smelled of cold ashes. There was a photograph of his father on the mantelpiece, posing with his racing bike and his Oakleys on his forehead. Grinning foolishly, in my view. I wondered whether a man could prove capable of transforming a woman into a lesbian, something he would certainly have had to have done for a woman to renounce the male species forever. I found him a fascinating character. Each time I had set foot in this living room, I had walked over and gazed at this specimen in an effort to solve such a mystery: How could a man have demeaned himself so? He looked like the sort of guy who drank milk all day long. "Do you think you're capable of coming down so that we can talk?" I called out over my shoulder as I examined the picture of the strange individual. "I need to have a word with you, believe it or not."

Gossips claimed that the heart attack his father had suffered about ten years previously was due not to natural causes, but to taking drugs while climbing the Col du Galibier.

I was a rumormonger. There was absolutely no proof that A.-M.'s veering out of control could, for some reason, be put down to this man's behavior. I had promised myself I would question her on the subject, but I had not yet done so. I was unsure whether we would have reached a sufficient level of intimacy to address the matter.

I wondered whether Jérémie asked himself the same questions I asked myself about his father, about the kind of husband he had been for A.-M.

What kind of father had he been? What kind of father had I myself been? I turned toward the staircase, at the foot of which a rather uninteresting green plant stood on a small table, and I tried again: "Well, Jérémie, my boy, d'you think I've got all night?"

A.-M. arrived on the first flight of the morning, when the dawn had just broken and it was still cold and the sky still blue. I immediately assured her that Jérémie had pulled through, but had not yet woken up, and I drove her to the hospital as the first shafts of sunlight gleamed over the surrounding mountains—the peak of the Rhune glowed as it emerged from the shadows.

I spared her the details. I spared her the blood. I spared her the vomiting. I did not let her know that I had found him dead drunk—and, what's more, unable to bleed properly, having chosen a knife that was as jagged as a handsaw with which to end his days.

In spite of everything, she was trembling. In spite of the fact that I had chosen my words carefully, she was biting her lips. She let me talk, nodding her approval as I listed the various initiatives I had taken during this tragic night, but she had not uttered more than a word or two since we had

left the airport, staring dumbfounded at the road ahead. Delicate blue clouds flitted above the sea, in the direction of the Côte des Basques.

I took her hands once we had sat down in the waiting room—opposite a young girl in a miniskirt, her eyes lined with kohl, who was breast-feeding her baby as she chewed gum relentlessly.

I leaned over toward A.-M. "It'll be all right," I told her. "Don't worry." She had just seen her son behind a glass partition, unconscious and on a drip, having spent a sleepless night at Orly in order to catch the first flight, and so I had taken her by the arm and led her over to a chair.

She had lived through ten years in the space of a few hours. Her skin was wrinkled, her complexion had grown pale. "He's not the first to do that," I said, in an effort to try and dissolve the drama. "The number of young people who are unhappy with themselves and who do that, they're legion. When they become aware that this entire life is nothing but a farce, etc. Not everyone is able to accept it without batting an eyelid. It's the most clearheaded who pay the price, that's the way it is, A.-M., and there's nothing we can do about it. It's always been like that and it will never change."

She wasn't listening to me, she was just weeping silently. The girl was now walking up and down with the child, who was also crying—squealing like a piglet being strangled. "It's my milk," she snapped as she passed close to me. "It's like water."

◆

Talking to Judith, Roger said that, whether I meant to or not, I had saved the boy's life, and my wife replied that she agreed.

I gave a slight smile. My role had been limited to calling the emergency services while the blood continued to flow from his arm. I had also switched off the music. Joy Division or not.

After the meal, I fell asleep at my desk instead of getting down to writing an introduction for a new edition of some of my short stories, illustrated by Tomi Ungerer. I had not slept a wink all night. I crashed out.

I had promised A.-M. that I wouldn't leave her son until she was back, and I was true to my word. I had spent the whole night pacing the corridors—the thought of Judith being unsupervised preventing me from falling asleep—and I was paying the price in the middle of the afternoon, dozing on my leather sofa, surrounded by my books, my DVDs, my music, my computers, my pens, my medicaments.

To transport this sofa, which I had inherited from my aunt, to my study upstairs had required the combined efforts of four local moving men, who were built like wardrobes—men who spent their spare time tossing tree trunks or carrying rocks for fun. I don't know whether it was because Hemingway had fallen asleep upon it on various occasions, during the time that he stayed at my relative's home, but I felt perfectly happy with it. I liked its smell. I liked the way it had aged. I never hesitated to sit down on it to scribble a few pages or to read the newspaper, but the best thing one could do was to sleep there.

On the very evening that Johanna discovered I had slept with my editor, this sofa had become my bed until matters were sorted out, and I had found it comfortable. I was convinced that everything would work out eventually because my feelings for her were unaffected, whatever she may have thought. I had hunched my shoulders, waiting impatiently for the crisis to be over, while Johanna shot me a black glance every time our paths crossed in one room or another.

I had not been granted permission to return to the marital bed before death took her, I had not had this good fortune, and the wound was taking a long time to heal. I despaired of seeing it heal. Twelve years later, the scar still seemed just as fresh. The recovery was making no progress.

I dozed. A.-M. called to say that she needed to speak to me. I put it off until later. I went downstairs. My eyelids were still too heavy for me to be able to join in any discussion. I did manage, however, to drag myself over to the door that separated my wife's bedroom from mine. I put my ear to the panel. I heard nothing. Feeling irritated, I peered through the keyhole. Her bed was empty. My heart leaped. Then I realized that, contrary to what I had thought, she hadn't stayed out all night. For it was not morning, but midafternoon. I climbed back into my dismal sheets.

Dusk was falling when I decided to get up. I bumped into Roger, who was going upstairs to put his daughters to bed. Lucie-Anne was perched on his shoulders, Anne-Lucie was holding his hand. He was in the midst of telling them something funny.

The guy had exceptional talent. You had to be strong-minded to stand up the way he was doing now to the misfortune that had hit us, to have such a fresh complexion, such bright eyes, such a thoughtless tone of voice. I had buttonholed Judith on this matter a few days earlier, and she said that she could see no point in wallowing in grief.

So, was I wallowing in grief? Was finding it hard to smile wallowing in grief? Was a lack of energy wallowing in grief?

I sometimes wondered about what the aftereffects could be on a mind that Roger had put to the test in the past. More than once I had found him semiconscious—and I was truly shocked that my daughter had fallen into the clutches of such a person—once, on the tiled floor of the bathroom, on another occasion wrapped up in the living room carpet, and yet another time halfway down the stairs that led to the cellar where I kept a few bottles of wine, foaming at the mouth, and with one hand stretched out toward my dry whites, which he had been unable to reach.

Marriage had revived him. It wasn't my opinion, of course, but I very soon had to admit that the boy was resourceful and that he had reembarked, if not on the right track, at least on one that was expected of a relatively responsible family man. For months, while I was living my great romance with Judith, I waited in anxious expectation to be told of a disaster concerning them, but there was no call from either the hospital or the police. Did that mean that Roger had emerged unscathed from his excesses at that time? From the numerous substances with which he had dosed himself? I asked myself this whenever he put on a show of cheerfulness or explained to me what we might expect with the price of a barrel of oil costing over two hundred dollars. I asked myself whether he was all right when I saw him stop in front of a shop selling surfboards or the window of a well-known chocolate maker. I wondered whether he was in his right mind since, personally, there was nothing I wanted.

I found Judith downstairs. I didn't understand Spanish, but I understood that she was talking about a property that Karl Lagerfeld had sold, on the outskirts of the town. Some figures were being exchanged.

I had married a businesswoman. I had not been aware of this to begin with, for I was her first customer, but the evidence was there. She now earned far more money than I did and the slight influence I had had over her to begin with, as a cult writer whose books were published by the best houses, had now vanished into thin air. I no longer impressed her.

To such an extent that my books were piled up on her bedside table, within easy reach, ready to be read, caressed, devoured. I told her I couldn't care less. That the days were too short. That I wasn't angry with her in the slightest. But she insisted on keeping them near her because she was going to get down to reading them at the first opportunity.

I didn't claim to be a man who was very easy to live with; no sane-minded woman can be particularly thrilled to share a writer's life for very long. I did not claim to be able to give her everything a woman had a right to expect. Very well. But did that exonerate her from a minimum of consideration toward me? Had she decided to spare me nothing? Was it a matter of revenge, of a desire to make me suffer?

Dusk was falling. I walked over to the coffee machine. Glancing up at Judith, I had the impression she was ending her conversation with a murmur.

"Everything fine?" I asked.

"Everything's fine," she said.

The evening breeze was getting up, the moon was shining. As far as I was concerned, her expression had become impenetrable. She didn't hesitate now to look me up and down. She enjoyed using her faultless Spanish in my presence. So as to taunt me?

However much I might thoroughly deserve it, it wasn't very kind of her to treat me so unceremoniously, to foist her view of the facts on me without the slightest precaution, without any serious explanation for her going out, her absences, etc.—not to mention that studio apartment she had rented in San Sebastián.

When I thought about it, I had to admit that we knew nothing about other people's suffering, that there was nothing we could measure it by, that we could be surprised, amazed, stunned by the damage we caused others. It was like killing someone with a punch in a street fight. Basically, I knew nothing about the harm I had done her. I didn't know whether she was repaying me a hundredfold or whether I still had a long way to go.

"Have you any recent news?" she asked.

"No, I was asleep."

"Poor woman."

"Absolutely. He really lays it on. With him, she gets to see every shade of color. Did I tell you how he had sprayed the bathroom walls with blood?"

"Yes."

"The ceiling reminded me of a Jackson Pollock."

"You've already told me that. Don't go on, I can see the scene all too clearly."

She made a gesture indicating that she had to listen to her messages. She now settled the majority of our bills. She claimed that it didn't matter at all to her. And that it would be out of pure and foolish pride that I would take offense. But I could see very well the pleasure she took in being in charge, in paying the suppliers, in slipping a check in an envelope without showing the slightest reaction, in giving the numbers on her card in a steady voice. With a wave of her hand, she could have the roof redone or change the garden furniture without having to ask me about our financial situation. I wondered whether I had not begun to lose her from that very moment, if I had not fallen from grace the day she caught me unawares choking on my sales figures.

With the telephone glued to her ear, she made a few notes in her monstrous diary—swollen as a cow's belly. Did it occur to her to think of Alice occasionally? I didn't want to make anyone feel guilty, but was I not justified in asking myself the question? Judith thrived. Quite simply. I had to grit my teeth not to let slip a slightly hurtful comment on the subject. Or was it I who was going mad?

A.-M. leaped to her feet when she saw me arrive. "It's dreadful. I was about to doze off," she said.

"How is he?"

This time, the waiting room was empty. This part of the hospital appeared to be deserted—apart from the two girls on duty in reception and a dark-skinned man who was rhythmically sweeping the corridor.

Jérémie had woken up in the late afternoon and then fallen asleep after a few minutes, but everything was fine, given the circumstances. In a weak voice, he had asked his mother to bring him his CD player on her next visit. I, too, considered this a good sign. Having said that, I didn't particularly want to see him.

"Let's not disturb him," I said.

She shook her head. We were obliged to walk, heads lowered, hugging the walls of the corridors, as far as the room. "Follow me," she said. Mothers are ever thus.

But I stayed at the foot of the bed, in the background, watching A.-M.'s face fall and harden like an old lump of fat over the pale mask of her sleeping son. There was a strong medicinal smell in the room. I stood there stiffly and silently, my head slightly bowed, wondering what it was she wanted to talk to me about.

If she didn't understand the reason why her son had been hanging around the local gays, I didn't really know what I could do for her. What exactly did she expect from me? That I should interfere in their affairs? That I should get involved in all that? Out of the corner of my eye, I watched the sickle moon hovering in the distance, above the dark, glistening pine trees of Chiberta. Reflecting that this wretched woman and I went back a long way, had spent time together, sitting on school benches. Reflecting on those years. And on this shriveled shadow, today. They were not a happy sight, the two of them. Both of them seemed to have come straight out of a crypt.

"Francis, I think your daughter is in hiding," she announced, without beating about the bush, as we were sitting in the waiting room, neither seen nor attended to. Since I did not react, she continued: "I believe Alice is alive and that she is in hiding. Unfortunately, I don't know where."

Due to the events that had taken place here and that had required her to come back urgently, A.-M. had not had time to pursue her inquiry further. She had at least been able to resume her research in light of this ransom demand that neither Roger nor the police had disclosed, and she had reached the conclusion that this entire story did not exactly hold water.

"I shall spare you the loose ends, the unanswered questions, the inconsistencies I've come across," she sighed with a shrug of her shoulders. "None of that rings true, Francis. I don't believe anyone has abducted her. Do you want to see my notes?" I didn't want to see her notes. I wanted to listen to her. I wanted to continue staring at that mouth that was uttering such marvels. Such ripples, such eddies, such currents. I nodded. I allowed her to finish. Then I stood up without a word and went for a walk along the shore. Completely deserted, at this time, even though it was still very warm and the wind had died down.

It was vital that I go back. I was in a vile mood. I was convinced that Judith was going to take advantage of my absence. Nothing was going to stop her. Jérémie would not be up to much for several days and A.-M. had categorically refused to tail her—something that had given rise to a rather lively exchange between us, but she hadn't given in.

The sky was dull and overcast. I didn't know what to wear. More precisely, I was incapable of concentrating on the choice provided by a wardrobe that was appropriate to the climate of the Île-de-France region, one that was far less pleasant and far sadder. Just as I was standing there with my arm reaching out at a handful of ties, Judith entered my bedroom and examined them before selecting some. I glanced at her to see whether I could detect a sparkle in her expression; I wanted to see whether my departure lightened up her manner in some way or other, but she played her cards very close to her chest.

"Once again, I hope you know what you are doing," she said quietly.

I replied with a look of impatience. We had discussed the matter at length the previous evening, until she had begun to yawn. We had thrashed it out. Given the brilliance of their previous investigations, I could obviously no longer have any confidence in Roger or the police. The question did not arise. I reckoned it was pointless to go back over it, and yet a part of me was holding back, a part of me refused to leave this house, things being as they were.

Looking at her watch, she decided to go with me to the airport. I packed my suitcase.

"I suppose there's nothing that can make you change your mind . . . ," she said to me as we waited for the plane in the evening light.

I took a room at the Hyatt—the bathrooms there were superb and very soothing, particularly since I planned to put the bill down to my general expenses. I ordered a club sandwich and some sparkling water.

Their apartment was close by. To kill time—A.-M. had advised me against doing anything before midnight—I was watching, in the semidarkness, after my hot bath, a TV channel that showed nothing but fashion shows. Occasionally, the camera drifted over to a party in which one came across some well-known faces, and over which a muted hysteria hovered, with bad music and certain substances that did not always turn out to be of the best quality, but which circulated in sufficient quantity.

Those who did not get caught up in that world deserved credit; and those who escaped from it, even more so. In that respect, Alice and Roger had worked a miracle. All of a sudden they had acquired a sense of responsibility. Working in a bank—even though it was a family business—and working as an actress required one to observe a certain number of rules: managing to get up in the morning, for example, not disappearing in the middle of a shoot, being worth your fee, etc.

But even though I had felt anxious about it all for a time, when they had just started, it was probably because I had forgotten that Alice had her feet on the ground. I didn't know anybody who was so profoundly pragmatic. However much I had gone on about it.

I missed her. I hoped I would discover something quickly. I hoped that something, at least, had begun to happen. That nothing could stop. That my path would lead me to my daughter, directly to her, without further delay. I hoped for it with all my heart because, should the opposite occur, I could expect to spend a particularly grueling winter. If I discovered nothing, if I returned empty-handed, if I did not come across a clue, if I searched this apartment in vain, then I could expect a complete breakdown.

Why was she in hiding, to begin with? No doubt it was better for her to be in hiding than dead—she could go into hiding a thousand times over—but that didn't answer the question. I knew her marriage was in a bad way—like father, like daughter—and that she was rumored to be having a few affairs on location. Was this the direction to pursue? Was she frightened of something? Of someone? Was she locked in a cellar? In an attic? Was she hiding deep in the forest? In this city? In this country?

The list of questions I managed to ask myself seemed endless.

One bright, crystal-clear winter morning, my telephone rang. Lake Geneva was sparkling like an electric field. Johanna and Olga were in town. Alice was about fourteen and it was her school calling. It's never good when the school calls.

I thought that she had broken a leg or twisted her neck because she had left on a skiing trip, but this wasn't the case at all. The school was calling for me to come and collect her at once. "Your little pest!" said the headmistress when she saw me. "Take her away immediately." A woman six feet three inches tall, with gray hair cut in a Joan of Arc style.

The class had arrived at the hotel in the late evening and the giantess was sending Alice home the very next morning. An awfully short stay.

"My wife and I dressed her from head to toe," I protested. "For the occasion. Tights, ski suit, après-ski wear, etc. Specially for this vacation."

"My dear man, I realize that."

"Listen, I'm not sure you do."

"I run a school, sir. Not a boarding house for wild animals."

"I'll pay for all the repairs."

"You will pay for them, believe me. And we are suspending her from school for a month. And if this happens again, she will be expelled for good."

Outside her office window, snow-covered trees rose up toward the blue sky while others ran down toward the lake in neat processions.

"I should like to know," I said, "I should like to know how my daughter was able to purchase two bottles of vodka. I should like you to enlighten me on this point. I think it may be necessary to warn other parents, because if Alice was able to do so . . ."

"Oh well, I know that she's very crafty. And that she's ready to do anything to get what she wants."

"Don't start beating about the bush. Please. Don't try to avoid the issue. Okay? Now answer me. Are you not supposed to protect our children? Are you not supposed to erect a barrier between them and the sale of alcohol? Would you not say that it's the minimum that we, as parents, might expect from you? Today it's vodka, but tomorrow it'll be drugs. It's you who should be punished. What's more, it's very simple, I shall talk to my lawyer about this. Enough pleasantries between us. I shall ask him to look after our problem as a matter of urgency. To be incisive."

Spaghetti was her favorite food, and it was what she mainly ate. I could easily imagine her preparing a tomato-sauce recipe along with a few of her chums in their bedroom. Smoking cigarettes. Telling each other their adventures. Being excited. Talking loudly.

"Have you ever been plastered during your life, dear lady?" I asked as I glimpsed Alice crossing the courtyard, dragging her heavy suitcase.

"That is not the question, sir."

I turned around and walked away.

I did not really understand Olga, my elder girl, who was four years older and who clung fiercely to her mother from a very early age. On the other hand, I got on much better with Alice. "Let's spare your mother the details," I told her. "You see, I think they're going to have to repaint everything. The ceiling, too. I shall have to write a short story just to cover that. In any case, I won't get away with a poem, you can be sure of that."

At midnight, I got out of the bath and dressed. More than two months after she had disappeared, people were still talking about her, about this young actress of whom nothing had been heard for seventy-eight days. Her photograph had appeared on the screen before I had had time to press the remote-control button. Looking puzzled, the announcer described several murders and kidnappings of young women that had occurred recently.

My daughter had married a young banker. She lived in an enormous duplex apartment, on the top floor of a building for which I knew the entry code. I spent the night with them from time to time, when I was in town. I had a key. I don't say they had put a key at my disposal. Let's not exaggerate. This was a key to the service entrance. Which I was not meant to take away with me, but to keep for when they needed it, in a drawer in my study, should anything whatsoever happen.

As a general rule, I did not abuse their hospitality. Not that they made me feel unwelcome—there was an adjoining studio apartment that provided a certain independence— but I frequently found myself spending the evening in the company of the babysitter and the children. Not that I wanted, at all costs, anyone to bother about me. Not that I did not understand that a young couple had better things to do than spend the evening with me. Nevertheless, I sometimes felt like asking the babysitter whether there was something odd about my hair or whether I was dressed oddly or if my remarks were becoming incoherent—but the poor girl already had an anxious expression on her face at the idea of being shut away with a man whose hair was going dangerously gray.

I took with me a flashlight, a camera, and a hard disk. Nothing else. I crossed the street. I walked round the square. At the corner, a man was building a cardboard hut beneath a bus shelter—his shopping cart was parked by the doorway. Our eyes met, then I made my way into the building. The entrance hall was deserted. After glancing around, I walked over toward the service staircase. I went up.

I entered the apartment through a sort of storage room in which brooms and shopping trolleys were kept—as well as the shoe-cleaning box. I shone my flashlight and made my way along the dark corridor.

I had no wish to be caught rummaging around my daughter's apartment. This absurd fear—for the situation demanded that I compromise my principles—guided my steps toward the curtains, which I drew.

I switched on the household computer and began to copy everything. This stirred some very bad memories in me, but A.-M. was convinced that the key to this business was to be found in this apartment. She had drilled this into me for two days and I had to trust her instinct. She had been in this job for some thirty years. Thirty years in which her instinct had become sharpened, to the extent that she had attained a second sight that enabled her to assert—insofar as the business in hand was concerned—that the key to the mystery was to be found inside this duplex apartment that I was obliged to go through with a fine-tooth comb. I gazed at her questioningly each time, but eventually she prevailed, persuading me that she had acquired this gift, this flair that only the most perfect detectives possessed.

I went upstairs and inspected the bedrooms, which I photographed methodically; A.-M. reckoned that I might miss certain details. Going through Alice's wardrobe proved to be a depressing and demanding task, however; her scent hung heavily and a number of the outfits took me back to very precise moments, to places where we had stayed; as I touched the material, I noticed, incidentally, that she had kept some clothes that had belonged to her mother and her sister, though I had never seen her wear any of them, at least not in my presence.

There was total silence—not a sound came from the street, due to the double glazing. I felt very nervous. In the old days, it would have taken rather more to affect me, but the tragedy that had unfolded before my eyes—and that was forever etched in my memory—had shaken me, made me more fragile. Certain particularly moving photographs of her previous life, which she kept in a drawer in her bedside table, quivered in my hand.

I noticed that their bed was soft, for I had had to sit down. I was literally shivering at the thought that fate, having removed half of my family, might now be depriving me of all of it. Was there no limit to human suffering? It was a king-size bed. I stroked the space where my daughter's shoulders fitted; her neck, often so tense. This acting profession was a loathsome one. I've always said so. But the girls went crazy before they realized it—and I was frightened that Alice might not be one of those destined to escape from it. She was a little too involved, in my view. But what did that matter now? I would not have made a fuss if she had been returned to me alive. I would have kissed the Lord's feet, without a moment's hesitation.

I considered lying down for a second. But I stood up and went downstairs.

I picked up cushions, opened drawers, had a close look at the bookshelves, rummaged in the wastepaper basket, looked to see whether anything had been concealed under the desk or in some dark corner, reached to the tops of cupboards, lifted up the rugs, photographed every square foot with a watchmaker's precision, etc.

I found nothing. Nothing gleamed at me in the darkness. On the other hand, I hoped to be able to gather together enough material to present to A.-M. and allow her to spot what I had not seen, what had been staring me in the face—I really did want her to do this. I set about in a methodical fashion. As the dark night wore on, at an hour when virtually everyone was asleep, I took the opportunity of a visit to the fridge to pour myself a large glass of pulp-filled orange juice.

Until the moment I heard a creaking sound. I froze. Switched off my flashlight. My brain began to work at great speed.

The door of the studio apartment opened onto a silhouette, a shadow play—the darkness prevented me from seeing more—that started to walk down the flight of steps that led to the living room. I squatted down behind an armchair. I regretted not having brought a weapon with me, even if it had only been a knife. Coming across a screwball was not unusual these days, indeed it was all too frequent; people have always said of me that I was a pessimistic writer, but I only had to read the newspapers, to look around me, listen to the radio; there were countless opportunities to meet a serial killer, the place was crawling with them, and I'm really not exaggerating.

The shadow passed in front of me. I immediately stood up, holding my breath. "Alice?" I mumbled.

Six months later, I had still not spoken to her. There was a strong probability, furthermore, that I might never exchange a single word with her. Nevertheless, I passed the handset to Judith, who, contrary to my wishes, had not broken off relations entirely with my daughter and Roger, and I left without waiting any longer.

The first spring days were sunny. The hydrangeas were in bloom. Since Jérémie was now employed doing maintenance work at the golf course, I no longer had him at my disposal to follow my wife and catch her in the act. So I was casting around in total darkness as far as that was concerned.

I was disillusioned. The feelings I had felt for both of them had grown numb, and this sense of emptiness was so intense that it deadened me. I had spent the winter giving lectures in different European countries to recover my breath, but I had expended a great deal of rather pointless energy; in Stockholm, the president of the PEN club had taken me on a round of the bars, from which I did not recover until the following evening . . . in Copenhagen, my editor clicked his heels as he raised his glass and looked me full in the eyes . . . in Vienna I knew some theater people, and God knows where they dragged me off to after my readings, making the most of my stressed, weakened state and the cold euphoria in which they immersed me. Reading made one thirsty. Reading properly made one very thirsty. I saw all too clearly the shining path of the alcoholic writer opening up before me; I saw how everything could become straightforward and within easy reach—to begin with at least. I had come back in time, too late no doubt to prevent Judith from making some important decisions on my behalf, but in time not to contract a liver complaint, possibly jaundice, during my tour.

"The girls send you a hug," she announced. I stiffened

slightly. "Me too," I replied. "Tell them that I send both of them a hug."

With my jaws clenched, I stared at the horizon. I didn't intend blaming Judith for having kept in touch with Alice and her banker, regardless of how I felt about them. One had to think about the little girls—with those two raging lunatics looking after them. The twins represented the one compelling reason not to end our relationship with the two screwballs who were bringing them up—and Judith performed perfectly well in the role that consisted of behaving as though nothing had happened, as though one should automatically turn the other cheek, whereas I personally was incapable of that, I was too closely involved, and it was a hard thing to admit to. At the age of sixty-one, it was becoming painful to recognize that one was unable to take a sufficiently dispassionate view, to display detachment, distance. Unfortunately, there was nothing I could do about it.

For the time being, I was returning from a tour in the former East Germany, feeling particularly calm and levelheaded; I had traveled the length and breadth of the country by train, from one city to another, and I had spent the majority of my time sleeping in first-class seats, closing my eyes, and opening them again five hundred kilometers farther on. I removed my shoes. The train is an excellent restorative. In certain cases, the train proved to be a real blessing. Piling up the mileage, keeping on the move.

I continued unpacking my bag and putting my things

away while she talked about the fact that she was going away shortly. Whom did she think she was fooling by claiming it was a coincidence? Well, let it pass. Be that as it may—and there we have the proof, the perfect illustration that crime pays—Alice was leaving for two weeks in Australia, on location, and nothing would comfort her so much as to entrust Lucie-Anne and Anne-Lucie to their grandmother.

My daughter had no shame. I had sniggered when Judith had told me about it. Then I had replied that I had nothing against it so long as I was not involved—so long as none of this concerned me.

Alice ought to know that there was nothing more she could ask me from then on. I had thrown the things she had left here into a suitcase, jumbled together, and once I had gotten a grip on myself, I had them sent to her. I no longer wanted to see anything that belonged to her in this house. I had asked Judith not to discuss my decision. I had begged her not to. I wasn't joking. She had shaken her head. She had sighed. She knew very well what a blow it had been to me. She took it upon herself—without my even mentioning it—to put the DVDs, the magazines, the photographs, out of my sight. I was comforted, at least, to have married a woman who did not instinctively seek confrontations— Alice was more than enough.

I was sorry that she was going away so soon. I had hoped that on my return we might spend a few days together despite the wretched path our relationship was taking—had taken. I was too optimistic. She had told Roger she would arrive the following day. Not that I would have had any specific suggestion to make about how to deal with our breakdown; I reckoned that the ordeal we were experiencing was insurmountable and that I was the first to have been wounded, but I wanted to preserve what was left, I was determined to do so. As long as it was still possible, I mean.

"Do they wonder whether we have a life?" I grumbled. "Does it occur to them, those two good-for-nothings?" I walked over to the doorway that separated our bedrooms. In hers, which was better situated, you could see the sun piercing the curtains and dappling its walls. I should have liked to have been able to tell her just how desolate I felt, but in the face of so much absurdity only a stream of air came from my lips. With time, I had come to understand that our actions were irreversible. One did not rewind.

I went with her to the market. "Do you have anything to say to me?" I asked her as she was examining a lettuce. She gave a look of astonishment. I came to her rescue: "Have you met someone?"

I could hear myself speaking, but it wasn't me. She shook her head and laughed. "But what on earth are you talking about? What on earth has come over you?"

I asked the boy the price of his lettuce and I paid him.

"Forget what I've just said to you," I told her as I walked up the central aisle. "My mind isn't very clear yet. I'm saying just anything."

She stopped and stared at me suspiciously.

I was not so naïve as to think that it was enough just to ask her the question. I didn't expect to see the truth come bursting forth like a spring in the midst of a bed of roses. Any more than I attached the slightest value to the disdainful silence with which she countered my pitiful assumptions.

"Forgive me," I told her. "But it's because of them. Ever since then, I see evil everywhere."

She looked around her before transferring her attention to me. "How can you still be dwelling on it?" she sighed. "Even today. After six months . . ."

"Time's got nothing to do with it."

"Of course it has. Francis, of course it has. Or else you're not normal."

I gritted my teeth. "She knew I wouldn't be able to bear it."

She continued to look at me for a moment, then she turned away and started to choose a melon. I was sorry I hadn't stayed an extra day in Leipzig so as to get dead drunk and come back home to find the house empty on my return.

Jérémie passed by on the other side of the street, sitting astride his lawn mower, and we waved at one another. Large numbers of seagulls were drifting in the sky. He parked his machine behind the hedge after he had loaded a packet of magazines I had kept specially for him onto the vehicle. "You've just lost your job," I told him. "She's gone away for a couple of weeks." He greeted the news with a satisfied smile.

"You're wasting your time with this," he said. "I've already told you. I've never discovered a thing. You're on the wrong track."

"Never mind. I'm not annoyed with you. She's a terribly cunning woman."

Glancing down, my eyes fell on his grazed fists.

"I'll tell you how it's going to end up," I said. "I'll tell you. When they get fed up with having you on their backs—and I'm sure that day's not far off—they'll grab hold of you. You can bet they will. That's how it's going to end up. With all the gays of the neighborhood after you. Precisely. Jérémie, I come across them every morning in the gym and I would not like those guys to corner me in the changing rooms with arms like theirs."

He could not care a damn. He was not afraid of being beaten up, he said.

I shrugged my shoulders. "Your mother's tired at the moment. Why not look after her a bit?"

"She's not tired. She's been dumped."

"She doesn't need any further shocks, I imagine. Be a little charitable. She worries about you."

Our children gave us plenty of problems, one had to admit. It was not simply a coincidence. The families that were spared were few. It was not surprising that A.-M.

should have vacillated after he had slit his veins open. Not many mothers could have coped with it. Not many mothers who had recently been dumped could have coped.

She was not so old. But within a few months, her face looked stricken, her complexion had turned gray. Every surveillance job grew more difficult, she told me. Standing on her feet for hours killed her. Her ankles swelled up. I had advised her to go on a course of high-dosage vitamin C and magnesium. To no effect, apparently.

He cooked her steaks, which she only nibbled at. Otherwise, he didn't pay much attention to her. The trials and tribulations of his mother's love life made him feel ill, he claimed. If there was one thing that made him totally ashamed, it was his mother and her warped tastes. "And I'm meant to feel sorry for her? I'm meant to comfort her? What she does disgusts me."

It seemed quite clear that he couldn't cope with his mother's homosexuality, it wasn't necessary to hark back to it; I could understand him.

Three days later the doctors informed A.-M. that she was suffering from cancer. Of a serious form. The X-rays were dreadful. "That's all I needed," she sighed.

She swore me to silence. She didn't want Jérémie to know. Then her gaze became lost in space and she shook her head for a long moment.

◆

Johanna's mother died from one of those lightning attacks of cancer that made you feel like a straw in the wind and that then tore you apart.

Olga and Alice, then aged twelve and eight respectively, were not very keen on going to kiss the remains of their grandmother, in her coffin, and on that day it made them feel downright frightened. The atmosphere was very strained.

The atmosphere was very strained as far as my in-laws were concerned, and for them the behavior of my daughters provided edifying and pitiful confirmation that I was not the type of man they had hoped for Johanna. Reading certain of my novels had not improved matters. And so, just as we were making light of the family incident at the back of the room, I heard voices taking offense at my lack of authority and condemning my obvious failure in terms of education.

Seeing Johanna's expression, I eventually leaned over toward the girls. "Sorry, but your mother doesn't know where to put herself. I'll come with you, if you like. Be brave."

Gloomy eyes were staring at us—assholes for the most part. But Johanna did not want to quarrel with them, nor endure their opprobrium, and since it was not for me to give my opinion on the matter, without any qualms I behaved in the way that she had advised me to from the very beginning, which consisted in avoiding confrontation and not annoying them. I had understood the importance these things represented for Johanna. I also knew what an ordeal this would be for the two little girls; I knew the magnitude of the effort that was being asked of them. The air seemed to be vibrating around us. Olga lowered her head. As for Alice, she suddenly stepped forward decisively.

We stood in front of the coffin. Holding their hands in mine, I gave each of them a quick glance. "I'm proud of you," I mumbled. "Well done. There's just one last thing we have to do. You'll be fine, girls. Be brave."

Alice was the smallest. I carried her. Their poor grandmother's face looked like a rotten lemon; she had fallen on the stairs while she was in a terminal stage, and she had smashed her jaw. Even I winced.

Olga appeared petrified. As for Alice, she leaned over without any hesitation and placed her lips on the old powdered cheek. Alice was already Alice.

"I did it for you, too," she confided to me a little while later.

"You amazed me. Your sister and I, I want you to believe me, looked at one another in silence. Mouths agog. You astounded us. I'm telling you. If you hadn't done that, I don't know whether I would have done so myself. Brrr! I've still got goose pimples, haven't you?"

The next in line, a vague cousin, was bleating like a calf about to be slaughtered.

Johanna joined us outside and thanked me as she hugged

the children to her. They were like that in the South, she apologized. They were sensitive about ritual and very fussy about it being observed. I expressed my opinion without comment. I had already had to give way on the question of baptism or risk being treated like a leper and held at arm's length, something that Johanna could not have accepted.

These people could not care less whether I was a writer or whether they heard me speaking on the television or the radio, literature did not impress them, and my income, which was still fairly sparse at that time, made them smile; whereas other people would have thrown their cloak in the mud so that I could cross the street without dirtying my shoes. But they were much rarer.

I could be a writer, or a scriptwriter, or a fireman, or a juggler, it mattered little, as long as I did not deviate from the path they had trod, as long as I kissed their dead ones while making the sign of the cross and passed down the codes of behavior to my children.

I carried Alice on my shoulders—she had certainly deserved it. Still full of admiration for the way she had turned the situation around to our advantage—along the path from the cemetery, we were now collecting our full share of satisfied smiles—I kissed the palm of her hand. The autumn was mild, for some days the trees had been a blaze of color, exceptionally sharp and bright, with their incredible reds and dazzling golds.

◆

Had I dreamed all that? Had I not woven the deepest relationship there can be with her, forged in the furnace of our distress? Had I been dreaming?

I began to think so. Be that as it may, I now knew that if she had to choose between me and her career, she would not spend very long on the question. I should draw the obvious conclusions.

I had never thought that such a terrible thing could ever happen. I had made the mistake of believing that certain terrains remained firm and solid, and could withstand wind and tide. I had shown great naïveté in this regard, sidereal blindness. At any moment, the ground can give way beneath your feet, whereas in my case I had imagined some chimera of terra firma, some nauseating El Dorado that was supposed to provide me with a little inspiration. As a result, everything was in place to provide the painful landing I had made six months ago, at the very moment that she had turned toward me in her wretched duplex apartment, on that deathly pale and mind-blowing night—as a result, there had been nothing left.

A postcard arrived from Australia. I didn't pay it a moment's attention and left it in the box, prey to all the drafts, at the entrance to the garden. It only required a slight storm and the mail was ruined. The ink of the best fountain pens could not withstand it, and still less felt pens, which did not last three seconds on the sodden stand.

Judith rang me in the late afternoon, as she did every day, so as to make sure that I was not allowing myself to die of hunger and was not neglecting the house—our cleaning girl had left us to follow her fiancé to Scotland and to work on a salmon farm. I did not leave anything in a mess.

I now had this secret to keep. In addition to my own family troubles. I was not allowed to speak to Jérémie about it, nor to anyone else. I tried to imagine this boy suddenly made an orphan and not one scenario appeared satisfactory, not one bright light shone on the horizon. And since it wasn't even certain that A.-M. would survive the summer—galloping cancer—the dark horizon was growing ever closer.

This job—which I had found for him by making three telephone calls—would probably not last forever. Agreed, spending one's life on a lawn mower did not constitute an ideal life, of course, but did Jérémie give the slightest sign that he could aspire to anything else? Was he much more than a child? Was not holding up a service station, in broad daylight, on his own, a fair indication of immaturity?

But did I have time to bother myself with this problem? Did I *still* have time to bother myself with *any* problem?

I thought of starting to write a novel in order to erect a wall around myself; I thought about it seriously. Over the years, I had developed the knack, by means of a few articles, a few vague short stories, of appearing busier than I actually was, but today, in *this* situation, returning to a novel seemed to be a requirement. The hardship involved seemed to be a requirement. Writing a novel demanded such energy that everything else became secondary. That was the advantage.

I had often had this experience. I had written my most recent novels as if I were building a fortress, and circumstances appeared to suggest that it was time to summon up these powers again, even if it might ruffle a few feathers. I had written these novels in the form of a forest, from which there was no escape: when Johanna died, I had begun to write the first pages of a book that would eventually contain one thousand, and the exercise had helped me keep my head above water, I freely admit; it had not always been easy, some days turned out to be bleaker than death, emptier than the streets of Hiroshima on August 6 at 8:16, 2 seconds, local time, more barren than an ice floe; but I had held the dogs and their jaws at bay and had otherwise enjoyed mixed fortunes in the bookshops.

Unfortunately, Jérémie passed my windows every day, perched on his lawn mower—he looked like a giant riding a child's tractor—so it wasn't very easy for me to wipe him from my memory. I could hear him coming from afar, a whistling noise that alerted me that the boy was in the vicinity. Occasionally, I would lie down on the floor or flatten myself against a wall, but that didn't alter matters very much.

A.-M. was apparently deteriorating before our very eyes, but her expression had never been so sparkling. I held my breath as I awaited her request, anticipating the blow that would come crashing down on me, but how to avoid it?

Jérémie was not an easy case, no, far from it. The other day, she had spoken to me about the brawls he regularly sparked off, the confrontations he went in search of—like a dog seeking its bone—as soon as it grew dark, and which were not just directed at homosexuals and those like them, but anyone who happened to be in his path. "He's right to keep it simple," I had said in a matter-of-fact tone.

Now that A.-M. had lost quite a lot of weight, my memories were reignited. Images returned. Now, I recognized her *almost definitely*. I saw her once more, surrounded by all those girls we went around with at the time, among that group whose faces and figures had become hazy; I was now even pretty well convinced that we had slept together. A.-M. and I had never reached that precise point—we had drawn a sort of heavy curtain over it—but I vaguely felt that there was an old bond between us. Watching her die was particularly painful for me.

"I'll do what I can," I told her. "But don't ask me to do more. Don't ask me to go beyond myself. Please. I'm beginning to get a bit old, you know."

"Never, Francis. I'd never dare ask you such a thing, do you hear?"

"Why not? What harm would there be? I'm answering you all the more frankly, A.-M., because you know my situation. Other matters are on my mind at the moment, as you well know. You have a ringside seat."

"Do you think I don't realize? You've already done so much for him."

I winced. She coughed slightly. Her lungs were riddled, the doctors maintained. Among the nurses, it was said that they hadn't seen such appalling X-rays since Chernobyl. Her eyes had filled with tears. Given the little interest that Jérémie showed in her—he informed me that he had thought his mother had picked up a bad flu bug—one could say that she was not rewarded in return.

Each time I listened to Animal Collective's "Banshee Beat," I became aware that man was not merely destined to spread suffering and ugliness in the world. It was raining, it was bucketing down, but this music came close to the miraculous. There was a moment when one could not help putting down one's glass and starting to dance—thanking God that one was not living through war or famine—and swaying one's hips, releasing a smile of satisfaction.

It was getting increasingly difficult to preserve such moments. By and large, in my view, life was a painful business. I had not danced every day, if my memory serves me right. And so, since that's the way it was, I allowed myself to be carried away momentarily by the music—wiggling around like some kind of worm in an electric socket—while the rain streamed down the bay windows. It was already growing dark. How would we manage, I asked myself, if there were no music? I had opened a good bottle of white wine.

I had not danced once since Johanna's death. Not *really*

danced. I had not married Judith in order to dance, but so as not to die. I had asked no more than that. Now, it was being thrown back in my face. It really did one good to dance sometimes. I did not intend to stand on ceremony. I was the only living person in this house. The music seeped into me through the base of the skull and ran down through my feet to disappear into the ground. Over the sea, there were heavy patches of black sky. Which collided. Which straddled the horizon. And when the disc was finished, I put it on again at the beginning.

One evening, Jérémie and I were sitting at the bar when he suddenly attacked a slightly drunken fellow who was moaning about his wife—who was seeking a divorce. It was a brief fight because the man turned out to be overexcitable, and he actually gave Jérémie a severe hiding before we managed to control him and chuck him outside.

I couldn't get over the way in which Jérémie had hurled himself at the man, apparently without thinking. The guy had in any case greeted him with a right full in the face that had literally stopped Jérémie in his tracks—and had put him in a position to receive the next blow. Total madness. He fell to his knees with a vague smile on his face, while his opponent thumped him again.

There was probably nothing to be surprised about in all this. A.-M. kept me regularly informed about these outbursts, but it was another matter to be part of it, to see it with one's own eyes.

I made him sit down on a kitchen stool and brought him various medicaments to treat his bruises. His face was red. Within a few hours, it would turn black—later would come the violet, the green, then the yellow.

"Keep them all," I said to him after he had finished. "Keep them with you. I think you're going to need them."

He very soon brought me proof that I had good intuition. The manager of the golf club eventually called me to say that despite his wish to be on good terms with me, he would not be able to keep Jérémie any longer. Not in the state he was in. Not with this swollen face, these grazed fists, the strange countenance that upset many people.

"Listen, old friend," I sighed. "OK. You win. I agree. I agree to take part in your literary festival. You have my word. I'll come and sign my books. I will sit behind a stall. Take it as done, old friend." I could hear him breathing on the other end of the phone. "His mother is on the point of death," I added—letting him understand that a kind of curse would come down on anyone who darkened the last light in her windows, on anyone who cast a shadow, in one way or another.

I gained a few months. Or, rather, Jérémie gained them. Although nothing was definite; it probably required one or two further complaints for the man to go back on his promise and get rid of the boy right away.

Meanwhile, Alice imagined that a few postcards from Australia would suffice, but I let them pile up in the mailbox without even reading them. For me it was a source of additional amazement to realize that she thought it still possible, still conceivable, etc., that she could resume some sort of relationship with me.

Judith, too, thought as much. But she had the excuse of knowing me far less well than my daughter knew me. I thought of Alice leaning over a balcony in Sydney, while a flight of gigantic bats emerged from between the tower blocks above her, leaning forward and scribbling a few words that were supposed to soothe me. Whom was she fooling?

Judith reckoned that of the two of us I was the one who paid the greater price, a fact I did not dispute, but this did not necessarily make me feel any more inclined to redress the matter. I did not discuss prices. Whatever it was, I accepted. That had nothing to do with the silent stubbornness that Judith conjured up in the course of our telephone conversations between the seaside and the capital. It was not stubbornness. It was a simple observation. There was no possibility of anything at all. This had nothing to do with stubbornness. With mere stubbornness.

She was still in a quandary. I could imagine her pouting. The weather in Paris wasn't great, she told me. Her granddaughters were exhausting her. She asked me about how my writing was getting on but was obviously not much concerned to hear my reply. The witch. I could have written *War and Peace* or *On the Road* and her mind would still have wandered.

Her lack of interest in my work proved to be particularly hurtful. Eleven years ago, when we first met, she was one of my most enthusiastic admirers and she would have listened to me in rapt attention if I had talked about how the novel I was writing was going. She would have listened to me with almost embarrassing enthusiasm.

Losing a reader was an unpleasant experience. If it so happened that this reader was also the woman with whom you lived, the bill was all the steeper.

"Take it from me," I said to Jérémie on the way to the hospital. "Losing a reader is worse than being given a hundred lashes of a whip. Losing a reader is a terrible punishment."

He nodded feebly. It was not easy to explain how you could spend thirty years in front of a sheet of white paper, and still less that what propelled this madness was style—that pit, that prison, that hovel that made one allude to the absolute necessity of a sentence, its beauty, its hidden vibration, without batting an eyelid. If I read a few pages aloud to him, by way of demonstration, I had the feeling of being up against a wall, of having arrived at the gates of the desert.

A.-M. was sleeping. There was a new treatment that required her being in the hospital for a few days—and at least this treatment made her sleep a great deal. As the evening drew in, we stood at the foot of her bed. She was asleep, yet getting her son this far had not been straightforward—he had said no to begin with.

We were talking in low voices. The corridors of the hospital were emptying. A.-M.'s room was equipped with a television set, which that evening was broadcasting images of a region that we would have to decide to bomb if we wished to guarantee our security. We were shown some maps. Things appeared to be simple.

There was a strong chance that in the fairly near future this world would be inhabited solely by murderers and madmen. The way things were going.

When the program drew to an end—over the glazed features of its presenter, who was unsure whether to close her eyes or bite her lips—we decided to leave. Somewhat depressed. "That girl has a problem," I said.

I nevertheless gave him a few tips concerning the attitude he ought to adopt if he did not want to bring down the wrath of his employer—emphasizing that having a job, these days, was no small thing.

"You frighten people. It's not difficult to understand. They must think: 'With a face like that, this guy is certainly going to mug us in a bush.' Have you looked at yourself? Have you still got a bit of common sense left?"

If they examined his hands, his swollen fingers, his raw knuckles—his gashed wrists—some people would run a mile.

Spring was approaching. Alice had extended her stay in Australia and Judith, as a consequence, had extended hers.

I woke at dawn, in the coolness and damp air. Then I immediately settled down to work. I slipped on a dressing gown and would sit down at my desk, set back from the window, or on the sofa. Writing a novel was absorbing. The last one I had written was about ten years ago and it had seemed to me that there would not be another one.

An excellent novel, as it happens. I had not thought I could do better, until now. I still did not think so, what is more, but the desire had returned. Much to my surprise. The desire to write a novel. Caught out at my own game.

It would actually have been better to stop at a success. I should actually have pulled out and rested on my laurels with articles and stories that did no harm to my image. But reason had nothing to do with it. When you are bitten by the demon of literature, what difference can an ounce of reason make?

My agent called me from New York, my publisher sent me friendly messages. But I felt they only half-believed me: how often had I repeated that I no longer intended to run over long distances?

There were many who thought that Johanna's death had broken me and no one would have staked a penny on my chances of getting back to the forefront. Possibly. It could very well be that I was broken and totally finished as a novelist. That would not have surprised me. It was still too early to tell.

Nothing was harder than writing a novel. No other human task demanded so much effort, so much self-denial, such stamina. No painter, no composer was in the same league as a novelist. Everybody knew this only too well.

I had sometimes gritted my teeth so tightly in the midst of a sentence that the entire room began to sing. Hemingway said the same thing. The grass did not grow green of its own accord. The landscape did not drift by on the other side of the windowpane by magic.

I should have preferred to resume normal relations with my daughter or start afresh with Judith, but writing a novel still seemed to be the most feasible thing to do in this case. Each passing day convinced me more and more. Nothing else appeared to be within reach. It was my last hope. I looked to the left, I looked to the right, and I saw nothing. I had never before started to write a book in this frame of mind.

About six months after the accident, with the arrival of the first snow, early in the morning on New Year's Day, I decided to set to work again.

We had moved home, and I now had a view over the

lake—a wonderfully strange and disturbing thing for a writer of fiction.

Once the evening had drawn in, I hadn't felt capable of writing anything at all. Alice had a fairly large bedroom at her disposal at the far end of the apartment and she made a lot of noise, but she was not responsible for the total loss of concentration I had shown over twelve hours at a stretch. The same thing happened the following day.

And throughout this time, a few feet away, Alice lay sprawled on her bed or rolled on the carpet without my being aware of anything.

I, too, found it difficult to overcome the loss of Johanna and Olga. I couldn't bring myself to say anything to her when I found her drunk or stoned. Quite often we would end up in tears, the two of us—which was not the best solution for our problems.

So in addition to this there was my terrifying inability to concentrate on work for more than a minute, to write more than the few lines that regularly ended up in the wastepaper basket once it grew dark; in the morning, I would wake up, feeling drained and as weak as if I'd written ten thousand words nonstop.

Being unable to write put me in a panic. Each day I was rooted to the spot between two doors, as if I'd been stabbed, or else I was unable to get out of my chair and I'd get bogged down.

When Alice and I happened to share the odd meal together, I would tell her about my difficulties while she nodded off over her bowl of cereal with red berries. She was deaf and I was totally blind.

Sometimes I even found myself looking at her and not recognizing her. One February morning, in the kitchen, as I was watching her, I noticed that she had goose pimples— even though she was wearing several sweaters—and that her breath was turning into white vapor. Puzzled, I placed my hand on the radiators, the huge cast-iron radiators, and they were freezing.

The thermometer showed 28°F in the apartment. I could not believe it. Twenty-eight. The same temperature as outside. And she said nothing. She was allowing herself to die of cold.

It was a worrying spectacle. I turned toward the sink. The hot water was running cold. I suddenly remembered the storm that had burst three days earlier; standing in front of the open window, I had hoped that a bolt of lightning would strike me and bring me back to life. Averting my gaze, I rose to my feet.

The fuses in the boiler had blown. This meant that Alice had been washing herself in cold water for several days—if she ever washed. I was appalled. A zombie. My daughter had become a zombie.

I dashed off to town in search of fuses. Was she feeding herself, at least? Did she get any sleep? I preferred not to think about it. The right thing to do would be not to have taken my eyes off her even for a minute, but that had not been possible. There had been Johanna's death, and now this: being unable to pull myself together, being unable to start writing again, as if I were lacking the arm that held the pen, the legs to keep going. I realized just how badly I had fulfilled my role as father, just how badly I had failed to protect her—was she not there at that very moment, her teeth chattering, in an apartment that had become an icebox, obviously high and barely able to stand up?

On my return, I hastily replaced the fuses and relit the boiler. The burner roared once more. I went and knocked on her bedroom door. Nothing. No answer. The streetlamps lit up the apartment from outside, but Alice's bedroom was as dark as a cave. I hardly ever had reason to go in, but I had glimpsed the room occasionally during my comings and goings—in search of inspiration or God knows what—so that I was not altogether surprised when, pushing open the door, I saw nothing initially, because it was too dark.

The shutters were closed. The walls were plastered with pages cut out of magazines: actors, musicians, artists, and the rest. The ceiling, too.

"Where's the light?" I asked.

"What is it?" came a voice from the back of the room. "What do you want?"

"I've come to find out how you are," I said. "Let me see you. Have you heard the good news? Haven't you noticed anything, these past few days?"

From the sofa where he lay, her boyfriend, Roger, groaned. I had actually never seen this boy in a normal state. Seldom on his feet, in any case. That he was a banker was the only thing I knew about him, apart from the fact that he wasn't violent with Alice. But I never managed to exchange the slightest word with him. We would slow down when we encountered one another—we'd break into a kind of motionless ballet—but without really stopping.

"Is he all right?" I asked, walking over to the bed, where my daughter was huddled up beneath a pile of blankets; I had the impression that I'd heard a death rattle coming from the throat of the said Roger.

She winced. "How do you manage?"

"How do I manage what, Alice?"

"You're dressed in a shirt. In this cold. What are you thinking of?"

"Listen, it's unimportant. Forget it. It's not what I'm wearing that I want to talk to you about. But much more serious matters. May I sit down?"

She immediately sat up, clearly irritated. I sat down nevertheless—even though I wasn't invited to do so—on the edge of her bed. She was shivering.

"I can't do it anymore," I said. "Bloody hell, Alice. I can't write anymore. Don't ask me why, I haven't a clue. I've spent one month writing three pages, do you realize? I'm doing my best not to shout, you know."

"But what are you talking about?"

"Don't tell me it's like riding a bicycle, Alice. Spare me such nonsense. I'm really down in the dumps, you know."

She sighed.

"What?" I persisted. "It's as if I was dead, isn't it? Isn't it just as if I was dead?"

She stretched out a feverish hand toward her bedside table to take a cigarette. Not only was she shivering, but her nose was running.

I took Jérémie to choose a dog. The idea had come to mind when I became aware that my writing work would now make me less available. He didn't say a word and looked straight ahead. The road ran between the pine trees. He had put on his safety belt and was twiddling his hands. "Come on now, don't be so nervous," I said to him.

The kennels were about twenty kilometers inland, in the woods, and the closer we came, the more Jérémie shrunk into his seat like some fearful old man. I watched him out of the corner of my eye as we drove in the direction of the Pyrenees and I felt as if I was driving him to his first romantic rendezvous.

I did not know much about this side of him, as a matter of fact. About his relationship with women. I didn't know what had gone on during those six years behind prison walls. And I didn't want to know. I had never brought up this subject with him. A.-M. had spoken to me about a girl before the service station episode, but the trail had gone no farther. She didn't know whether they had slept together, whether they had been in love with one another or anything like that, because as soon as she had the misfortune to inquire a little deeper, he exploded. He yelled at her. He held her responsible for everything that had gone wrong, starting with the death of his father, whom she—the ultimate in despicable behavior, he barked at her—had left for the love of a woman.

I hoped that the dog was a good idea. I was going to have to devote much more of my time to my office and I could already imagine Jérémie prowling around outside my windows if I were seen to be doing nothing, calling out to me to tell me of his arrival; starting a novel was the hardest bit, the riskiest part of the exercise, and it required the full attention and all the energy of the person at the controls.

A twenty-five-kilo bag of dry roast-meat dog food lay prominently on the backseat. My share in this business. My gift. Top-of-the-line dog food. "I'd advise a boxer," I said as we were passing through a forest of extraordinarily green oak trees. "If you see a boxer, take it. Listen to me, take it. The boxer is ideal. Intelligent, strong, devoted, affectionate, noble, etc. Especially if it's a bitch. So don't hesitate. You won't be disappointed."

I had phoned and they had put two aside for me, one of which they had brought from Lower Navarre, which was just three months old.

"Have you got something against boxers?" I asked to fill in the conversation. "You know what they are, at least? You won't be able to resist them, I promise you. And don't forget that they're smooth-haired animals. I won't go through the list of advantages of a smooth-haired domestic animal. You know them as well as I do. In any case, don't forget to give it a name this time."

The gates of the kennels appeared a few moments later, and they were wide open. I pulled up in the parking area and suggested that he get out, since no one was going to choose a dog for him.

The manager was a charming man who immediately invited us into his office. From outside came a cacophony of barking and mournful howls. He asked me to sign one of my novels, in very poor condition. It was because he had read it over and over again, he explained, so I forgave him for having turned down the corners of the pages and treated the jacket so roughly. When I told him that I was working on a new novel, he blushed and stammered. I hoped that I still had a few more readers like him around the world.

"I saw your daughter the other evening," he informed me, while Jérémie was inspecting the cages and winking at me. "On a television program. She's making a film with William Hurt, isn't she?"

"I don't know anything about it," I replied, stiffening imperceptibly. "I've not been informed."

"She spoke about you. About her admiration for you, for your work."

"That's what a father likes to hear," I said, looking elsewhere.

Jérémie had stopped a little farther away. He was sitting on his heels and staring at the inside of a cage. Yet again,

I found it hard to imagine this boy holding up a service station—and, what's more, causing the death of the checkout assistant. Although he had given me all the details, one evening—the hours spent behind the counter with the man, in the same pool of blood, up until the moment when, within a hair's breadth of being killed by the incensed policemen, he had given himself up—I still couldn't believe it. Even though there was not the slightest doubt about his active involvement in the reported incidents, I remained incredulous.

How could one begin to imagine this boy with a gun in his hand?

"She claims that you taught her how to cook."

"That's wrong. I didn't teach her a thing."

One morning, I removed all the postcards from my mailbox and chucked the whole lot in a garbage truck that was passing by.

On hearing of this, two days after she had returned from her stay in Paris, Judith couldn't believe that I hadn't even glanced at what my daughter had written to me. She couldn't get over it, she said. My hard-heartedness. My blindness.

"I know people more hard-hearted than me. Much more hard-hearted than me. Believe me. Listen. Judith. Good heavens. You're not *obliged* to be against me. It mustn't become a reflex, you know."

I did not see her again until the evening. She came up to my study and positioned herself in front of me, as dusk was falling, while I was trying to write a few lines.

"I'm sorry, but I'm not *automatically* against you. But I'm not going to say you're right when I think you're wrong, I hope you understand."

I looked up at her.

"If you're going to tell me I'm wrong," I said, "you would have to have all the information to hand. So that you can judge with full knowledge of the facts. Now, I'm sorry, but that is not the case. You're speaking without knowing."

I had spent part of the afternoon with problematic sentences. No one in the world had been as close to Alice as I had been and nothing irritated me more than when people seemed to think they could have an informed opinion about the relationship I had with my daughter—had we not already spent a lifetime together, had we not already made up our minds beforehand to spend our previous lives together?

"I don't intend to discuss it," I said. "If it's she who sends you, she's wasting your time. I should like you to understand that it's not stubbornness on my part, nor a question of pride. I should like to think that nothing is beyond repair, but let's be serious for a minute. How could I still have anything to do with a daughter who sacrifices her father to her career as an actress? You know, it almost makes me want to burst out laughing when I say these words, it hurts so much. But it's over for me. It's over with her. How could she have thought otherwise, in any case?"

She sat down on the Hemingway sofa, opposite me. The last beams of daylight streamed across the room.

She leaned over toward me. "Forgiving would make you seem stronger, Francis."

"Don't try that on. Don't try that with me. I couldn't care less about being strong. I don't want to be stronger. She has let me die on a slow burner, she has tortured me for months, knowing full well what I was going through. Not the tiniest compassion. This obsessive need for publicity. This need to succeed at all costs. At *any price*. Shit!"

She sighed. "But who has made them like that? Who has hardened them to such a degree?"

"I agree absolutely. But not all fathers have been treated as I have been treated. Not all fathers in this country have been left high and dry, I'm sure. Torn apart, I mean, dismembered."

We went down to eat. Passing the door to my study, I turned around and cast a last glance over the room in which I had spent the entire day struggling with myself, and it seemed as if I could feel the electricity that still hovered there, hear the inaudible crackling of the air. I closed the door quietly.

◆

The last time we had sex was several months ago. I did not attempt to keep a precise tally, it was depressing enough as it was.

That evening, however, we had it off, but it was strange. Not in the least disagreeable, but unusual, odd, and it reinforced my sense that she was giving herself to other men. I didn't know exactly what it was to do with, but their imprint was there, I could tell. And once the business was over, just as I was imagining myself collapsing quietly alongside her, she asked me to go back to my bedroom.

In the course of the week, I tried to persuade Jérémie to return to his surveillance task outside his hours of work and to report back to me once more on Judith's movements. There were few people, fortunately, who would not strive for an additional income in these times of slow growth on the west coast. Jérémie now had a dog to look after.

Ever since he had begun mowing the golf links, he smelled permanently of newly cut grass—and also of gasoline. I had the sense that he was struggling with himself less, that some of his tension was disappearing. It was not yet time to claim victory, but there was a light that was doing its best to glimmer; A.-M. declared that, in spite of her own wretched state of health, she was able to breathe more freely at last.

Not that he devoted any more of his time to her or appeared to be more solicitous, but he seemed to her to be less tense, less closed in on himself; he was totally engrossed by the young boxer bitch he had adopted—her very existence enthralled him and left him speechless. She observed him, A.-M. told me, from the armchair to which her cancer had assigned her and she witnessed the changes that I myself had noticed in her son.

"I hope he allows you to get on with your work," she had said to me.

"It's all right, don't worry. I know how to stand up for myself. Let's try not to live like savages."

A lifetime had passed between the time when I had probably slept with the girl and finding myself together with this woman in a hospital room, half dead already and in a state of limbo. In that instant, I discovered that life lasted for a split second.

"I'm glad you're getting back to writing a novel," she said to me. "It's the best thing you could do."

I grabbed hold of her two bags and walked toward the exit while she signed papers at the desk. Jérémie had slipped off. Watching her walk toward me across the parking lot, I felt doubtful about the treatment she had been given. When she sat down beside me, for the return journey, I was reminded of a shadow.

The doctors reckoned that it was too late to attempt anything else and that she would be much better off at home.

Jérémie had come by to ask me a favor, giving the excuse that he was busy due to an appointment with the vet.

So I drove her home. Jérémie was not marvelous at cleaning and, in the course of a few weeks, he had found a way of creating chaos in the house. The worst mess was in the kitchen. She clung to the side of the sink, shaky on her feet, to fully take in the spectacle.

I sighed silently and made her sit down at the table, which was entirely covered with cutlery, plates, bottles, and bits of leftover food that was rotten, shrivelled, or dried up. There was an unpleasant smell everywhere, the saucepans and frying pans had not been washed, the floor tiles were sticky, and there were packets and cartons left everywhere.

I wanted to clean things up a bit for her return home, but she stopped me immediately, with a sharp movement of her hand. "Please," she breathed, keeping her hand raised.

In her condition, and considering the extent of the task, I didn't think she would complete it before nightfall. Unless she took a pick-me-up.

Guilt gnawed away at her, more surely than did her cancer, and the latest eruption—Jérémie slitting open his veins—had literally ravaged her, stunned her, crushed her. So much so that she was unable to stand up to him, to impose any authority over him—if she ever had been. So she let herself die.

In early June, she weighed no more than forty kilos. "Your mother weighs no more than forty kilos," I informed her son.

◆

In spite of everything, she continued her inquiries. She hoped to put enough money aside to cover the burial costs and to increase the amount that would come to Jérémie once she had died.

I wondered what he would do with it. I personally thought that this money had a specific value and that one could not just allocate it to anything, that it had a sacred value—not to say a sentimental one—but the only response I got was a slight shrug of the shoulders. "In any case, don't trust a bank. See what happens. All these people whose savings have been swallowed up. Entire lifetimes of sacrifices and exertion. It's outrageous. You see all these houses for sale? I see them myself. That should make you cautious. That should make you think. Take a guy like Roger, for example. Could you have an atom of confidence in a man like that? Who would dream of entrusting their savings to him? Your mother's gone to a lot of trouble, old friend. Whatever you may think. And she's doing it for you. Not for them. Do you understand what I'm trying to say?"

He did not appear to. One part of his mind was concentrated deep within himself, whereas the other was focused almost entirely on his dog, from dawn till dusk, so that he paid virtually no attention to other matters, as if nothing else existed between these two poles.

"It doesn't matter. Don't trouble yourself," she told me. "Let him do what he wants with his money. It's all the same to me."

Her complexion was a yellowish gray. The slightest attempt to follow anyone exhausted her. She dabbed her clammy forehead. So much so that Judith, who had been in a quandary for a long time and reluctant to help, eventually took pity on her and sometimes invited her to share our meal.

Judith took Jérémie to task one morning; on the previous day in the evening, his mother had suddenly had a dizzy spell in our kitchen and, after attending to her and listening to her rapid breathing, we found her to be in a very weak condition. She told him that she preferred not having had a child if it meant being rewarded in that way and encountering such ingratitude, etc.

Jérémie stood rooted to the spot. He lowered his gaze. For some reason or other, his heart was always in his boots in Judith's presence. She damned well frightened him. One day when I showed surprise at this, he turned scarlet and began to mumble.

Judith certainly had a strong personality. I could testify to that. He felt paralyzed and her slightest remark made him feel as if he had reverted to childhood; I could vouch for this, it was taking place before my very eyes.

I knew that the lack of eagerness he had displayed about following her over the course of the past months had been to do with the hold she exerted over him. I knew this very well.

He was basically still an adolescent. The majority of boys of his age were little more than pathetic imbeciles, vapid and helpless, incapable of looking a woman in the eyes for more than two or three seconds, and I could see him cringe at the reproaches that she was leveling at him concerning his indifference, literally shrinking, retracting and shriveling as she bombarded him.

A few days later, returning from a dinner party with friends, we discovered a cardboard box in front of the door. Inside it was a cake. Carefully prepared, as the card inside stated, by Jérémie and his mother, who, on this occasion, had joined forces. I suggested we taste it. The night was clear, soft, and without a breath of wind, without any mosquitoes, without any insects, without any moths: their total disappearance had been one of the subjects discussed during the evening, as had the programmed death of the West and the invention of the water engine.

One week after Johanna and Olga were buried, I had sold our apartment, put our possessions in storage, and we had set off on our travels for several months.

On the day before our departure, at dusk—a time of day when I used to feel particularly exhausted, particularly empty, and unwell—Alice walked into my bedroom and found me sitting on the bed.

I knew that Johanna kept a diary. I knew where she kept it. But two full weeks had gone by and I had not picked it up. It required a certain degree of courage to shove my hand into her chest of drawers, to rummage among her things, among her underclothes, and I had not yet found this courage, this strength.

Alice hurled her mother's diary at my face. I soon understood the reason why. The cover of the diary cut my lip slightly before continuing its flight across the bedroom.

"You make me sick," she said to me.

"Very well," I replied.

This drive around Grisons was costing me dear. I withdrew to the bathroom and locked the door so that I could clean up the blood that had trickled down my chin without being disturbed. She immediately banged on the door, ordering me to open it. I turned on the cold-water tap and I was dabbing my lip while she started aiming solid kicks at the door and letting out long howls. "Baaaastard!" she yelled, hammering violently on this wretched door while my blood dripped, drop by drop, into the basin. "Open up, you baaaastard!"

The following day, when we set off for Sydney, she was wearing large dark glasses and had not uttered a word since she woke up. The shrink had advised us to travel together, to take a few months to rediscover ourselves and, my goodness, the whole thing was off to a very bad start. I was—even though she hadn't said so, she had certainly made me feel it—the last person in the world she wanted to be with.

I had a fairly good idea as to what she had been able to read about me, for I knew how her mother had taken the affair. Very badly. Very very badly. And Johanna was not a woman to mince her words.

I no longer had any chance of discovering from Olga how she would have viewed my conduct, but I doubted whether the scales would have tilted in my direction. The three women were against me. The three of them blamed me. The only one who was still alive wouldn't even speak to me.

As we were about to land at Singapore and I was looking forward to being able to smoke a cigarette or two, we entered some strong turbulence. The plane began to leap about amid the dark clouds. The in-flight meal trays were flying about before the air hostesses were able to collect them. People were yelling. Oxygen masks dropped down from the ceiling. In normal circumstances my teeth would have started to chatter, I would have taken up the crash position after being shown what to do, my face would have been contorted, etc., but not this time, this time I remained impassive, I couldn't have cared less about dying, I couldn't have given a damn about dying . . . instead I held out my arm resolutely across the row of empty seats—she had asked not to be seated right next to me and a cow at the Air France counter, a sexy blonde, had stared at me for a few seconds before granting her request.

As the plane plunged several thousand feet, the man sitting in front of me was screaming that we would all perish, but I kept my hand stretched out toward Alice, steadily held out, palm open, without flinching. As it fell, the Airbus roared and whistled like a kettle while my daughter cowered and wondered whether she should let go of the armrests and reach out to that lousy hand now—now that we were on the verge of death. I did not know whether she had understood that the fate of this plane was in her hands. That she only had to make a simple movement for this nightmare to be over.

It was as if we were in some crazy henhouse. What a din! What a commotion! Everything whirled and hurtled about. Sitting in their corner, the air hostesses gritted their teeth.

Yes, I had slept with my editor, Marlène Antenaga. Yes, I had done so. But I was far from home, in Grisons, I was drunk, and this woman ran one of the most prestigious publishing houses in the world—some would have killed their father and their mother to appear in its catalogue. This woman, Marlène Antenaga, could put a stop to a writer's career with a simple snap of her fingers. Should I therefore have taken my own life? Should I have said good-bye to the full-page ads and the long interviews she obtained for me when each of my novels was published? We had laughed so much as we walked back up to the chalet—I had downed a bottle of gin with Martin Suter and Robert McLiam Wilson. My wrist was aching from signing so many autographs. What a marvelous evening. The fragrance of the night air in Grisons. The sweet and distant whiff of the cowshed in the chill air. The narrow staircase that led to our bedrooms, beneath the eaves. The wonderful feather-filled eiderdowns. The mist flooding the valley. The bells around the necks of the cattle. The neutrality. The stone upon which Nietzsche came to sit and meditate.

◆

I had been a widower for just over a year when I pushed open the door of an estate agent in the center of town in search of a house, having decided that Alice and I could no longer live in the same place together—if I wanted to keep her alive, at least.

I looked up and it seemed as if I was gazing at a woman for the first time in ages.

During the days that followed, she arranged appointments for me and took me around in her car while Alice continued to get frequently and systematically stoned, accompanied by this banking kid with whom she had been going around for months now—the guy had been sick in the bathroom, burned the carpets, broken plates, alarmed the neighbors, walked around the apartment for nights on end; the guy was a real pain, I loathed him, but I didn't want Alice to run away, something she had threatened me with when one morning, just as I was having my breakfast, I saw this idiot appear from the end of the corridor, barely able to hold himself upright, as if he still had his needle stuck in his arm, and suddenly collapse on the table, sending my bowl of coffee flying, my fromage frais, my cereal, and what failed to hit me full in the face shattered on the tile floor and spilled over my feet, so I then became furious, I stood up, knocking my chair over, I wiped my face, threw down my napkin, then I grabbed the screwball by the neck and dragged him over to the landing, from where I was about to throw him down to the foot of the stairs, when she appeared, white as a ghost, she appeared and urged me on: "Do it," she said to me. "Go on, do it, and you'll never see me again, you bastard."

The insult had stuck, in spite of the months spent together here and there—and on account of the extreme cowardice I had displayed in order that things should not become worse than they were. Alice did not use the term every moment of the day—as she had during our visit to Sydney, by the end of which I'd come to think that "you bastard" had become my name—but she still used it on certain occasions. I looked at her before releasing the object of her concern, who had not been aware of anything and had collapsed into a bad-tempered coma. When you have only one daughter and do not want to lose her, the outcome of every battle is known beforehand.

This week spent crisscrossing the area in the company of this woman who took me to visit houses brought me abruptly back to life. After five hundred days of grieving that had sapped my energy, I woke up once more, blinking. She drove a Lexus—secondhand, she eventually admitted to me on the morning of the third day, by which time we were already on first-name terms, Judith, Francis, etc. "Business wasn't as good when I was driving my Honda Civic," she added with a laugh.

I was bowled over. I didn't understand what was happening to me straightaway. I was glad to be back in the Basque Country; to see the rays of sunlight glistening through the rain, to breathe the sea air, to drive through the forests, to rediscover the taste of chilies and goat cheese. But that wasn't all.

I played hard to please as far as choosing houses was concerned, pretending that I needed to see as many as possible before reaching a decision. I settled comfortably in the Lexus and let myself be driven all over the country-side, from the hinterland to the coast. Spring was coming, preceded by vast, crystal-clear skies. The craziest notions bombarded me.

She had read my books. All my books. I had the sense that I was living in a dream. "But above all, I love the way you write," she had added.

"A stroke of luck," I had thought, for this Judith was a very attractive woman, younger than me by about ten years and financially independent.

"You make me blush," I had said.

The following day, she suggested we visit a house beside the sea. Then she changed her mind. The house was ideal, but it was beyond the price range I had set. "A villa in the Andalusian style," she sighed. "I adore it. Frank Sinatra stayed there after the filming of *The Man with the Golden Arm,* which had literally exhausted him."

"Compared to Hemingway, why, Nelson Algren is not worth two pennies," I explained. "But let's go and take a look, in any case. Who knows?"

"Not on your life, Francis. I don't want to appear to have pushed you into anything. Don't go on about it . . ."

As soon as she drew up in front of the house in question, I knew it was the right one.

In the attic, I discovered an enormous room that would have ultimately persuaded me had I had the least doubt about the matter. I could already see where I would place my desk, the electric coffee machine, the sofa. I could already visualize myself at my computer, involved in the battle for literary prizes: Marlène Antenaga—it was fair play—had reinstated me among the firm's top authors on the very day of the burial, having embraced me and kissed me on both cheeks in front of members of the press who had announced that I was changing publishers a few days previously.

From the window, I could see the sea. "It's not Edmond Rostand's house," I said, "but it's not bad. It's not at all bad. The owner is mad, of course. He'll never get that much. But the house is really not bad."

We looked at one another.

"Marry me," I said to her. "You're my only hope."

I reeled at the notion of being in the presence of the wife I needed, in the house that I needed. At the notion of my recovery. I suddenly realized that my mouth was completely dry.

On the day that Roger had crushed his daughter's fingers by swinging on a solidly built rocking chair, he had sworn he would never touch drugs again. The accident occurred when he was completely stoned and was supposed to be looking after the twins. He had given up threatening to cut his hand off as he had originally planned to do, but he had taken advantage of my presence in Paris so that I could witness his entire stock being thrown down the lavatory without further ado and, to my total amazement, he appeared to have kept his word and Alice had done so, too.

Anne-Lucie was barely one year old when she had crawled over toward her imbecile of a father, who, in a final bout of crazed rocking, had rolled forward heavily, his hands firmly gripping the armrests, and had reduced her fingers to pulp; the fact that she had only lost two fingers was little short of a miracle. As for their mother, who was spending the weekend with the producer of an indigestible comedy she was preparing to make for television, she could hardly be excused for a large part of the responsibility in this appalling business.

Be that as it may, however, they had pulled themselves together and had managed to create a relatively normal family—something that had led me to temper my criticism and to tone down my sarcasm.

It had been touch and go for them. Unlike Judith, who had not had the good fortune to live in the same house as them at a time when the dealers and the emergency services were beating at my door, I nonetheless remained on my guard. Not, I stress again, that I would have refused to acknowledge the progress they had made—especially since

Judith and I, after three years of marriage, were hardly an example of perfect success.

There I was, lost in thought, daydreaming, while Judith was leafing through some travel brochures at the Air France counter, when their plane came down to land beneath a bank of heavy clouds, head-on to the wind that blew from the Bay of Biscay.

There were half a dozen photographers at Biarritz-Parme airport that morning. The sky was heavy with snow and the wind was gusting. According to the latest news, Alice was suspected of having an affair with one of these lousy actors and this had provoked a sort of buzz around her. Snowflakes the size of small nuts were fluttering over the runway. No sooner was she married—the twins were just two years old—no sooner had she got rid of her bad habits—she only took a few sleeping tablets from time to time, when the pressure was too great—than here she was trying something new, here she was discovering other experiences; sometimes I was glad I was merely her father.

In any case, we watched her arrive that morning, looking glorious, emerging from a flurry of snow—Christmas was fast approaching. Straightaway, the flashbulbs crackled. She adopted a few poses. After which, she walked over to us,

"You're looking good, both of you," she said in a husky voice as Roger and the twins—who had briefly been dispatched to collect the luggage—elbowed their way through the crowds toward us.

"Has Roger had some hair implants?" I asked, winking

in the direction of my son-in-law, who had just loaded three enormous suitcases and a few bags onto a cart.

"Of course not. He'd never do that," she answered in an exasperated voice.

"Oh good. Forgive me. I could have sworn that he had."

She herself was carrying several bags from smart boutiques—a perfume shop, a delicatessen, a chocolate maker—which I suggested relieving her of so that she could embrace Judith without crushing everything to bits.

By shoving a local radio microphone in front of her face, a girl with a large bosom, wearing small spectacles, markedly reduced the effusiveness.

Alice stared at her for a moment. "Thank you. But I don't want to make any comment. I have nothing to say. Please understand me. Brad is probably the nicest boy I know, but I repeat, to have a relationship with your partner is the surest way possible to end up as a second-rate actor. I'm delighted we've had such a success together. Let's leave the gossips, the fundamentalists, the envious, the scandal sheets, etc., to their dreary jobs, OK? My husband is here. My children are here. My parents are here. Do I look as if I have run away with my lover? Let's be serious. Soon people will start alleging I'm having an affair with Jack Nicholson. And how old is he now? Eighty? Good God! Listen, I'd just like to say one thing. Angelina is my friend. Listen, I know that for some people that doesn't mean very much. But for me, it does. Try to understand that."

I looked at her. She had put on some weight again, she

was radiant, she exuded health, energy, beauty. She had become, I fully realized as I watched her that morning, and without any possibility of being wrong—as the gusts of wind shook the shimmering eddies of dead leaves and blue-tinted snow behind the bay windows from which, in fine weather, you could normally see the Pyrenees—one of those loathsome young actresses who were self-confident and arrogant, and totally unbearable.

But it seemed to me that I preferred her like this rather than as a junkie or someone involved in a road accident; I was her father, I had no other choice, and so I didn't want any difficulties with her and I depended on time and introspection to save her soul.

For the time being, she was consumed by fervor, quite clearly. The poison had taken hold of her. All too often, actresses don't become people one would want to mix with until they are in their fifties, when the masks begin to slip.

Scarcely had she arrived than she shut herself in my study and remained there, glued to my phone for a good hour.

"I hope she's making a reverse-charge call," I remarked as I poked at a large beech log that was sparkling. "I hope my publishers aren't trying to get hold of me either. They have my direct line. They know they can call me at any time, day or night."

By way of a reaction, Roger let out a sort of groan. I looked up. We were alone, for Judith was putting the children to bed.

"Is everything all right?" I asked, finally taking note of his generally sorry appearance. I handed him a drink.

"It's all true," he sniggered. "It's all absolutely true, Francis. They spent a week together in a luxury hotel in Saint-Raphaël. Shit! She lies with every breath!"

I nodded silently. Then I looked up at him. "Even as a very little girl, she lied," I said. "It's dreadful."

There was always a price to pay if you went for a walk with a pretty girl on your arm. And if, for one reason or another, that pretty girl was even slightly well known—an actress, an heiress, a singer, model, television presenter, writer—it was better to take the joke coolly, better to break your heart before you walked through the door.

Two days later, succumbing to their impulsive ritual, some elderly arthritic swimmers threw themselves bravely into the frozen sea and emerged with a smile on their lips— even though they were that much closer to death—while Alice and I had breakfast in the silent house. Looking faintly amused, she watched me carefully butter the slices of toast. Her chin resting in the palms of her hands. Indolent. Alice's eyes were wide open, but her face was still asleep.

I had become hopeful again on the day I came across her in the kitchen, early in the morning, when I realized that we were out of the woods—at least, partly so.

The day was breaking and the pale light was giving way to a coppery glow—which must have had red in it somewhere—in which microscopic sparkling particles hovered. The wind had dropped completely. A fine layer of frost gleamed on the surface of the snowy carpet that covered the garden and was beginning to melt in the salt-filled air.

"First of all, let me inform you that you're not in a position to preach to me."

"I'm simply reporting back the remarks he made to me, I'm not judging your behavior."

We exchanged smiles.

"I don't know what's wrong with him," she said. "He wasn't like that in the old days."

"In the old days, you could have gone off for six months with whomsoever you liked without him noticing."

I squeezed some oranges and put some eggs on to boil while she stretched her limbs. I far preferred her like this, when she wasn't made up and was dressed only in a kind of T-shirt—ABUSE OF POWER COMES AS NO SURPRISE—and blue-and-black Chinese pajama bottoms, and when her hair was awry and she began to move, speak, breathe, and think like a normal person.

"I shouldn't tell you this, but I spent a marvelous week with him. He's incredibly handsome, isn't he? We didn't spend a moment apart. We gave ourselves a real holiday. Apart from you, nobody knew where I was. I hadn't felt so calm and free for ages."

"I know just what you mean, as you can imagine. Sometimes one just wants to go and lose oneself in the forest. Not to be answerable to anything, to be unable to be reached . . . But I get the feeling that Roger's not taking it as well as the other times . . . It's a long time, a week. I imagine that if Judith were to disappear into the arms of someone for a whole week, however lackluster our relationship these days, I would not exactly be pleased."

I served the eggs and sat down opposite her. Should we curse the heavens for what has been taken from us or give thanks for what we have been left?

"Let's eat before they get cold," I said.

"All OK, with Judith?"

I gave a slight shrug of the shoulders. Five long years had passed since Johanna's death and I hadn't really recovered. I had thought that marrying Judith would put an end to my suffering, but the illusion had not lasted very long and we had celebrated our third wedding anniversary at a luxury hotel in Normandy where I had had the poor taste to dissolve into tears.

"We make love in the dark," I said as I played with the yolk of my egg with my knife. "There's both positive and negative in that. Nevertheless, when I was setting off to water your mother's and your sister's graves the other day, she told me that she would not come to the cemetery with me from now on. She didn't need to explain why. That's what she said to me: 'I don't need to explain why.'"

My daughter took my hand for a moment—I never refused anyone warming the cockles of my heart when the occasion arose. I didn't know how we had managed to cross the abysses, negotiate the storms, endure the flames, in order to share the occasional morsel of food, but one thing was sure: she could not have coped without my help, just as I could not have coped without hers.

I would be unable to say at exactly what point she had begun to take herself seriously. What shift had occurred. So was what I thought funny not in fact so? Was it not tongue-in-cheek?

An actress's career is the worst a woman can choose. For herself and for those around her. And Alice had fallen into the trap, headfirst.

When she let go of my hand, I gave a start.

"I'm still waiting for the play you promised to write for me," she said to me.

"A play? Is that all? How could I have promised you such a thing? I don't manage more than ten pages."

"You promised me."

"Well, I must have been crazy. If I ever promised you such a thing, believe me, Alice, I must have been crazy. And incredibly conceited when the only talent I possess, nowadays, consists purely in knowing how to brush aside what shouldn't be done. That's fine, but there's not much to show for it. It doesn't open up great horizons for me."

"If you were really bothered about my career, you'd write it for me."

"Don't say that. Of course I bother about your career. From the day you were born, I've bothered about your career. So please don't tell me I'm not bothered about your career. Don't talk nonsense. As soon as I'm up to it, I'll write a dozen for you. More even. It's all I ask for. I'm prepared to espouse any religion to get the inspiration back, I'm prepared to pray to whatever God, provided the ability to string together five hundred thousand symbols with a beginning and an end were given to me again."

She nodded. She looked outside and then asked me what I had to clear the pathway with, for she felt in the mood to do some exercise.

All I could find for her were a shovel and a garden broom. People around here used to say that there was a far better chance of glimpsing the empress Eugénie's petticoats than of seeing snow fall in these parts.

She put on a tracksuit and set to work. It was an excellent initiative on her part, in view of the extreme ease with which I attracted every variety of sciatica, lumbago, neuralgia, etc., available. My first back pain had come on a few days after the accident and I had experienced many more since—which no massage was able to relieve anymore. Had I not been destroyed as a writer at least, I thought a little bitterly, it would not have been half so bad . . .

In any case, watching her shovel up all that heavy snow

instead delighted me, there being few opportunities for avoiding backache.

Her transition from teenager to being a woman had passed me by. And this person whom I saw bustling about my garden—efficient, rosy cheeked, fearless, breathing streams of pure vapor into the chilly air—I found it the hardest thing in the world to imagine that she had been a spark within me, even before her mother's involvement.

Roger woke me from my daydream. "Being in love with that woman is a curse," he groaned behind me. "She drives me around the bend."

"Roger? Hello. Slept well?"

He winced.

It was seven o'clock in the morning. I was going to pick up Jérémie from the police station. I was yawning, I had scarcely woken up, and I was still rubbing my eyes; I had worked very late, on a recalcitrant paragraph. Then I had collapsed onto my bed, dead weary, and the telephone had woken me with a start. The dawn was still clear and diaphanous, but a warm breeze was already moving in from the sea. In my job, if you gave in to a paragraph, if you didn't deal with the problem before going to bed, you couldn't climb the ladder, you condemned yourself to remaining a second-rate writer.

He was in a cell. Behind bars once more. The superintendent told me I had nothing to worry about and said I could take Jérémie away, but that I ought to warn the boy that here, between these walls, they didn't want to hear of him again.

"Make him listen to reason, Francis. I wish you well. Personally, I'm not so sure. I tell you, what goes on in the head of an eighteen-year-old lad who's capable of holding up a service station . . . that's pretty heavy stuff already. It's not like helping a blind person cross the street . . ."

I nodded in agreement.

"Don't let yourself get dragged into that," he advised me.

"There's no danger of that. I'm writing a novel. I don't have a moment to myself."

"That's fascinating. Writing a novel must be fascinating. Well, it fascinates me."

I nodded in agreement.

I came out accompanied by Jérémie. There was a café opposite. I needed a coffee so as to wake myself up properly; to bite into a creamy little pastry as a reward for having risen at the crack of dawn. I indicated to Jérémie that he should order whatever he wanted. His right eye looked like an Agen prune, his nose like a beefsteak tomato. His right hand was bandaged in a cloth or something. And the rising sun that illuminated him, covering him in a golden light, certainly didn't manage to improve matters.

Afterward, I took him straightaway to the pound and we retrieved his dog, which began to leap about all over the place, sending bits of slobber everywhere. We drove along the coast on the way back. Offshore from the casino, mounting their boards and shading their eyes from the sun, the first surfers of the day were scanning the still horizon, erect as prairie dogs. The sky was turning a deep blue. His dog was lying calmly for the time being, its tongue lolling over the backseat.

"I've decided not to give her a name," he mumbled. "I think it's silly, after all, to give an animal a name."

I didn't say anything. I pulled up outside his house and got out without waiting for him.

I found A.-M. in the drawing room, in the half light. "He's getting along fine. Stop worrying. Come on, it's over, it's already water under the bridge."

"It's lucky you're there, Francis. I can't even drive any longer, you know. I'm so frightened something might happen while I'm driving. I prefer to stop straightaway, that's how it is. And soon, I won't be able to walk anymore, I imagine. That'll be fun."

After she had drawn back a curtain, we watched in silence as Jérémie played with his dog outside the house. Out of the corner of my eye, I glimpsed the photo of his dead father on the mantelpiece, dressed in his cyclist gear, with his enigmatic expression—I had no desire to wink at him.

The neighbor was having his hedges clipped. The noise was unbearable. Even with the windows closed. Because of the erratic nature of the explosions of sound, there was no way one could get accustomed to the din—to the high-pitched screech of a moped—that the motor made. I hoped that someone would go and shoot this appalling gardener or stick his ghastly machine down his throat once and for all—I was ready to pay someone to do it—but no one came.

Silence fell again. Then the fellow suddenly turned on the gas again just at the moment I was getting ready to thank the Lord for having put an end to this torture. I was prepared to pay a certain amount of money for him to stop.

I wondered whether Hemingway would have gone and beaten him up. I was thinking of him because I had been re-reading "The Snows of Kilimanjaro" the previous evening, and I had been reflecting that he really was one of the best writers I knew. I thought as much each time I reread this story, no question. A superb writer. Powerful. Economical. Subtle. Pity he hadn't married my aunt as he had promised her he would—though he was mainly in love with Brett at the time.

There's a now well-known photograph in which he is wearing a loose-fitting white pullover, with a largely frayed collar, with cable stitching, and perfect for winter sports, and it was my aunt who had knitted this sweater for him. I'm not making it up. She knitted me an identical one before she died, which I never dared wear—but ever since then I had always written trying my best to be worthy of what I was doing.

I went out into the garden, blocking my ears, and went

straight up to the cause of the trouble and his stinking, noisy, long-handled machine that bristled with blades. The man was wearing a soundproof helmet. I tapped him on the shoulder. A plastic visor protected his face. He switched off the motor. When I realized that it was Jérémie, I turned on my heel, but he called out: "Are you angry?"

"Angry? Why should I be?"

"You haven't spoken a word to me for three days."

"That's another matter. That doesn't mean to say I'm angry. I'm not angry in the least. I've got nothing to say to you. It's not the same thing at all. I just wonder why we should continue to waste our time, you and I. Why should we waste our breath pointlessly? Since you don't listen to me. Since the only thing that interests you, just at the moment when your mother gets a little closer to death day by day, before your very eyes, is going for walks with your dog or coming home in the middle of the night with your face all bloody, or not coming back at all and ending up in the police station with all the nutcases and drunkards like you. What can I say about that? What can I say, at this stage? If you're all there. Listen, I begin to wonder whether you're taking your medicaments. I wonder whether you're not just making fun of us, Jérémie."

He swore that he was taking them. I had no way of checking. I shrugged my shoulders and returned home. I closed the bay window again. He looked in my direction without flinching. I stepped back and sat down in a chair, without taking my eyes off him.

◆

If one judged purely on the result, if one merely wanted to see the benefits of the scheming that had separated me from my daughter, I had to admit that the aim had been achieved: everything seemed to smile on her, professionally speaking.

It was difficult not to come across her on television or in magazines, not to hear her on the radio when I was stuck in a traffic jam, not to hear her voice, not to feel the blow full in the chest. You saw her everywhere. She was in a film made the previous summer by a former graduate of the National Film School and praised in the top film magazines, and plaudits had been raining down on her ever since she returned from Australia. Her dance card was filling up. Getting oneself talked about, by whatever means, appeared to be the right thing to do.

Sometimes, whenever Roger was in the picture, one couldn't avoid his satisfied, nonchalant air—still less the eager expression on his face when he announced, taking his time, that the rumors of separation, as far as their relationship was concerned, had never been so groundless.

It was probably the truth. At the end of the day, they were a close-knit team. Their relationship had withstood the various strains Alice put upon it—and got away with. They were an astonishing couple. It was the same thing every time, and I could not help remembering the occasion when they found it difficult to drag themselves out of bed, or felt too weak to climb on a stool to change a lightbulb—or simply close the door of the washing machine—and yet here they were, today, triumphant, attractive, relaxed, reaping what they had sown; they had trampled me underfoot, but then this generation loathed us, one had to come to terms with that.

Roger could appear as if he didn't care a damn about anything and Alice could seem resolutely determined. "I saved that fellow's life," I said to Judith, pointing to Roger with the tip of my knife. "Twice. Not once, two times. One evening, I prevented him from swallowing his own tongue. And on another evening, I drove across town with my foot on the pedal to take him to the emergency room. The miserable son of a bitch. Ruthless. Completely ruthless. I fed them. I gave them a roof over their heads. But for them, I was nothing more than a guy who fed them and gave them somewhere to live."

My appetite ruined, I pushed my plate away. "If you don't mind, I'm going to channel-hop," I said, getting to my feet to grab the remote control.

"Well, now I know," she said behind my back. "I know you're not going to change your mind. I wasn't absolutely sure. Now, I know."

"Did you think I was joking?"

"I thought you would calm down eventually. Really nice people calm down in due course."

"Good for them. Much good may it do them. Wonderful. I admire them enormously." I went back and sat opposite her. "Please. There's nothing we can do about it. Don't make things even harder for me. Please think of me a bit. I'm the victim in this business. Try not to forget it. Don't make life any more difficult than it is. Can't you see there's nothing I can do about it? Something in me refuses."

She lit a cigarette. I switched conversations. "Have you heard about this house along the coast for which a Russian just paid five million euros? That's over the top, isn't it?"

She stood up and took our plates away. I lowered my head. Instead of pouring oil, I was throwing sand.

I went into the kitchen and asked her to forgive me. Then, with a resolute step, I went back to work.

There was a squall during the night. A few low clouds, stacked up gloomily on the horizon, should have alerted us, as should the falling barometer pressure, but neither she nor I had paid attention. I leaped out of my reverie when a shutter slammed violently behind me. I was right in the middle of a sentence. I got up, however, and grabbed hold of it in order to attach it to its catch. All of a sudden, the wind began to howl. The vagaries of the weather in this part of the country were not worth mentioning. My clock was showing one o'clock in the morning.

I went downstairs. There was a draft blowing through the living room between the chimney and a French window that had been badly closed. Outside, the umbrella shade was about to fly away. I went out and was almost blown away with it. I had to lie flat on the ground with the umbrella and tie it up while sharp gusts of wind roared about over my head, tousling my hair. The chairs had rolled into the hydrangea bush, the table was teetering on its legs, I could see my irises blown flat, and there was lightning in the distance, toward the mountains, which were lit up for a brief instant. Yet no rumble of thunder could be heard. It was not raining. The drops of rain came from the sea; the foam was flying.

I got up to rescue the chairs. Judith came with me. I signaled to her to attend to the table, for the wind was growing ever stronger. It was no mean achievement to remain standing.

Over ten years, the wind had carried away one table and three umbrellas. A few dozen chairs.

After we had secured the garden furniture, the wind began to drop. There was a time when we would have enjoyed the piquancy of the situation, when our sense of humor would have easily outweighed everything else, but our eyes were downcast and we sighed silently. Then we went indoors.

"You're working late, these days," she said to me.

I was still feeling a bit dazed and light-headed. "Am I? Do you think so?"

"Mind you, it's not a criticism. It's a sign that everything's going fine, isn't it?"

"You can't say that. You can never say that. As you know. But OK, let's suppose it is. All I can tell you is this: I'm progressing. Page after page, plodding along. I push on. Day after day. What more can one hope for? Isn't that a miracle in itself?"

She looked amazed. I admired the casual way she had settled into an adulterous relationship, that impassive expression with which she met any outside attempt to discover what she was up to.

"I'm glad for you. I get the feeling that it's a good story."

I nodded vaguely. Then it rained heavily for five minutes.

"Does forgiveness exist in your religion?" she asked as she watched the sheets of steaming rain cascading down on the garden, beating against the bay windows.

"That depends on what it is. Living together means sharing certain values. Agreeing on the bounds beyond which you can't go. In that context, forgiveness exists."

With these words, I went outside, for the storm had stopped. A soft breeze began to blow, with the force of a hair dryer.

"You've often left, by the time I get up in the morning," I said.

"But I go to sleep before you do."

"That's true. But I can't work in the morning, as you know. Mornings are fine for young fathers."

The moon shone down now and the sky glittered as if nothing had happened.

"I can understand people being allergic to this climate," I said, examining my mud-covered moccasins. The air was filled with the smell of tamarisk, the scent of honeysuckle.

"Why should you be taking an interest in me once more?" she said in the half light.

"What do you mean?" I sniggered.

"I thought that we knew where we stood on this matter. I thought we had identified the problem a long time ago."

I cleared my throat. I had behaved so foolishly toward this woman that I didn't always find the words that would have allowed me to turn the conversation around. "Writing this book gets me worked up," I eventually admitted to her. "I'd forgotten what it was like. Don't pay any attention. You know, there are two possibilities: either it's worn me out, or it's the other way round. It doesn't surprise me you find me a bit strange. Sometimes, you know, without a couple of tetrazepam, I can't sleep a wink I'm so stressed. But I'm not complaining. I know that some people get ophthalmic migraines or eczema into the bargain."

"Francis, I'm being extremely serious."

"Oh Lord God!" I muttered, my head down, my fists clenched, my soul in shreds.

When I had decided to introduce Alice and Roger to Judith, I had organized one of those meals for which I hold the secret, in which everything goes wrong.

We were still at the planning stage. She had sold me this house, we had slept together six or seven times, and I was her favorite writer, which made her a relatively serious candidate to succeed Johanna—before I became totally crazy—but it was important that my daughter and her lunatic of a boyfriend did not cause her to flee on the spot.

I had decided to cook a mutton-and-vegetable stew but I couldn't find the casserole. I had asked for someone to give me a hand with the mountain of packing cases—Johanna's and Olga's belongings had accompanied us, adding pain to the confusion because everything had been jumbled together indiscriminately and their things suddenly began to appear at the top—but no one answered.

There was nothing unusual about that, in itself, since they were so often stoned that they slept most of the time, but without this casserole I couldn't achieve anything ambitious, whereas I ought to have been outdoing myself.

By the time evening came, I was distraught.

I had drunk half a bottle of white wine and I was thinking about the possibility of pouring myself some more as the risky aspect and the enormity of the undertaking loomed larger, as the sky grew dimmer, as the horizon shimmered weakly above the sea darkened by the twilight. The clock chimed eight o'clock. Not only was I asking myself how I could have organized such an encounter, given the challenge it represented, but I was equally astounded by the fact that I was thereby making our relationship official—something that had curiously and maddeningly escaped me up till then and that I now regarded as a further betrayal of Johanna. I had tears in my eyes.

I hoped that everything would cave in on me and bury me. Almost two years had passed, but I could not get out of my mind the fact that the last image she had taken away of me, and which I could no longer do anything about, was that of a man who had betrayed her. And here I was replacing her with another woman.

With any luck, Roger would bring out a needle in the middle of the meal or swallow a whole handful of drugs as Judith looked on in bewilderment. Neither was I entirely satisfied with my stew; not because I had not eventually laid my hands on the precious cast-iron pot, but for some strange reason that I couldn't be bothered to fathom, neither my turnips nor my carrots had caramelized as I wanted.

I had bought this unfamiliar house, and I wondered whether it was going to suit us. I didn't know a damn thing. I had laid the table and lit a few candles. A perfectly dismal atmosphere.

When the doorbell rang, I would have liked to put a bullet into my head or to have disappeared forevermore. I gave myself a final glance in the mirror before opening the door. I frightened myself.

"Hello," I said. She responded with a passionate embrace, which I barely saw coming, among the coat stands. I should have expected it. In retrospective fear, I imagined Alice's reaction at finding me in close contact with a woman other than Johanna and I led her stumbling along among the warren of packing cases that the movers had piled up in narrow canyons, in unsteady columns, in meandering stacks.

I sat her down on the sofa that I had inherited from my aunt, a real Basque woman and a lover of art and literature—a sofa that I was actually longing to have taken up to my study—then I bustled about filling our glasses. I smiled, but deep down winced bitterly, knowing what a huge mess we were heading straight toward.

I found her cruelly attractive that evening. Yet I could imagine only too well how distressed, flabbergasted, and astonished she would be by the end of this family meal I had so skillfully concocted; the awful food, the awful company.

"Do you and this house get along well together?"

"Perfectly well," I replied.

"Francis, I'm glad."

"Judith, I am, too."

"Where are they? I'm getting restless."

I winked to reassure her, already fairly drunk; best not to be completely sober when you are to be involved in your own ruination. I signaled to her to wait for me and I made my way to the stairs, which I immediately proceeded to climb, clinging to the banister.

Were they asleep? Were they going to tell me that they had forgotten our party, or would they simply refuse to take part just because there was nothing that compelled them to make the acquaintance of the "woman from the agency," as they would not fail to christen her?

I knocked at their bedroom door without the slightest hope, with a kind of morbid pleasure, but they came out immediately and walked out in front of me; I was in no state to run after them. Given the measure of the attraction I felt for this woman, I had considered myself justified in arranging such a meeting and I was now going to discover the cost of my error. Brazenness had a price. Arrogance had a price. Naïveté had a price. I jumped the last step unintentionally and almost landed flat on my face.

Having drunk a large glass of wine, I caught up with them in the kitchen, for everything was probably going to take place in the kitchen: the actual meeting, the unpleasant things, the cutting remarks, the hurtful things, etc.

All three of them were bent over my lamb stew as if it were a cradle—apart from the fact that it was steaming. It seemed an odd scene to me. Alice still had the wooden spoon in her hand. Roger was holding the lid. Judith turned toward me; I thought she was going to clap. "Wow!" she said.

I then noticed that Roger was wearing a clean shirt and that he had the look of someone else. That Alice had done up her hair in an elegant way. I stroked my chin. I took a step backward. "Papa, you're the best," Alice said to me. Roger agreed, giving me the thumbs-up sign.

Apart from me, everyone was hungry.

I sniggered aloud during the meal, but I wasn't able to break up the mood.

"I think we'll be getting married soon," I heard over

the dessert course. I glanced up at Alice. "But what's all this about?" I mumbled with difficulty. "I wasn't informed. You're going to what? Get married?"

Without waiting for an answer, I got up from the table, taking my glass with me, and went and sat down a short distance away. I pondered.

"Well, perhaps you won't be the only ones," I said. "All right then. Perhaps you won't be the only ones, after all. Perhaps it's best that way."

Judith burst out laughing. She pretended that I was very funny. I was in any case, to her mind, one of the funniest writers in the world.

The following day, she paid me a visit, I asked her to sit down, and she told me that she had spent a very pleasant evening.

I had been suffering from a violent migraine ever since I had woken up, but I greeted the news with a vague smile. Then came the moment where she gingerly brought up the subject of that announcement I had made the previous evening, concerning us, and whether it was serious or not. And if it was, whether that would necessarily pose a problem for Alice.

These days, A.-M. was taking morphine and rarely ever left home.

Most of the time, when he wasn't working, Jérémie

stayed outside, under the porch, together with his dog and his CD player, and only came in at night. I knew that he never addressed a word, so to speak, to his mother, and simply made sure that she had what she needed, fetching her a glass of water, switching off the lights, then heading straight upstairs with his dog at his heels without even re-moving his headphones for a second.

When I looked at him, I could still see so much anger seething inside this young man that I wondered whether the treatment he was being given served any purpose. "Strictly none," A.-M. confirmed. "Thank goodness he's got that dog with him. Thank goodness that dog's there, you know."

These days, she stayed in her slippers and hobbled around the ground floor accompanied by different carers and home helps who took over from one another at differ-ent times of the day and made her walk—except that she had nowhere else to go, she was fond of pointing out, and was consequently told off politely for her gloomy remarks.

"He wears gloves, you know."

"He wears gloves?"

"To touch me. He wears gloves to touch me."

She made comments like this, terrible ones, in a matter-of-fact tone of voice as she gazed into space. If Jérémie was there, she would position herself in the shade, by the win-dow, and look at him furtively while she questioned herself, in an astonishingly calm voice, about the total ingratitude of this son whom she had brought into the world and who wore gloves in order to touch her.

Spring was already well advanced and the Spanish property market, buzzing briskly, was taking up a great deal of Judith's time; the messages informing me that important business was retaining her on the other side of the Pyrenees increased. It was beginning to get hot and I saw her take only light outfits away with her. I watched her depart in the morning without being sure of seeing her in the evening; she waved from the gate and I raised my hand before going back to my novel.

How many writers had gone back to their novels rather than dash off in pursuit of their wives? The best ones, without any doubt. The clairvoyants. The great masters.

"I'll double the amount. Don't desert me, damn it! Jérémie, Jérémie, look at me. A few hours each day. When you've got a spare moment, perhaps, but I've got to know, you understand. Uncertainty gnaws away at me. It can't go on like this. Summer's coming. I'm going to go crazy, you realize. I'm in the middle of writing a novel. I can't interrupt myself every moment of the day to dwell on my personal problems. This time, my reputation's at stake. I'm risking my all. What's more, if this doesn't go well, I'll stop. I won't write another line. I'm telling you. The return on the investment is too small. One thing's for sure, in any case, I can't allow myself to make a mess of my comeback, Jérémie. I must keep my head clear. Oh, I know very well what you think.

That I don't appear to be doing a job that's too demanding. You're not the only one, you know. But I'm not complaining. Have you ever heard me complain? I know that many men are up with the dawn, I know that many men are exploited by their bosses, I know all that. I'm aware of all that. I know that there are men who see their fields devastated, their houses go up in a puff of smoke, their schools collapse, while I apparently just sit gazing up at the sky like a simpleton. Ha! Ha! I wish that writing could be as straightforward as dressmaking, I wish that writing could be as easy as it looks. Well, it isn't, actually. Don't believe that. Don't believe it's heaven-sent. I have to devote all my attention to it. I have to concentrate beyond what is reasonable. I can't let there be any questions that nibble away in my mind. Like an infernal bee buzzing around a flower bush. I can't, Jérémie. I can't put up with it, it's out of the question. Beyond my ability. I must know. I must liberate myself, rid myself of this terrible and obsessive uncertainty, do you hear, even if it's very unpleasant, even if it doesn't do me any good, do you hear, Jérémie?"

I had counted the days, now I no longer counted anything. The precise moment that Alice ceased to exist for me seemed such a long time ago nowadays, so distant, so deeply embedded in the limbo of my memory, that having taken root on the far side of a dark and bottomless ocean, it would strike me all the more clearly. "I know I shouldn't say this, but it's as if you were dead. I'm sorry."

I hung up. Mildly disconcerted. She hadn't attempted to speak to me for a long time—ever since the day when she got fed up with me putting the phone down without a word after she had begged me to say something, no matter what, which was still too much for my liking.

I walked to the seashore, feeling irritated and troubled. I didn't know what she wanted because I hadn't given her time to express herself, but her telephone call was so unexpected that my formerly uncontrollable reflexes had not been functioning. I had spoken to her. Probably in a somewhat curt manner, but I had nevertheless exchanged a few words with her and I had almost wanted to wash out my mouth in my handkerchief—and God knows how piqued I felt that such crude images should come so easily to mind, but Alice still triggered such harsh and primitive reactions in me.

I walked as far as Hendaye. I caught a train on the way back. My shoes were full of sand and my trousers were wet up to the knees, but I didn't exactly know what I had been up to. In any event, it seemed to me that I had not been thinking of very much. I flicked my tongue over my salt-covered lips. There was a strong smell of old tobacco in the compartment dating from the time that smoking was permitted.

◆

Alice wanted to inform me that she was pregnant. I learned about this the following day from Judith, who looked at me as if I was a monster—Judith, who always tried not to understand what motivated me.

"Will it be a boy or a girl?" I asked, yawning.

She gave me a piercing, chilly look. I had realized long ago that my fatal error had been not wanting a child. She had never forgiven me for it. That was how it still was today and barely a day or two passed without our having this kind of silent squabble. In every glance she shot at me, I could discern the void that the absence of a child had left in her. Unfortunately, my regrets were of no use; my nonregrets were of no use.

"It makes no difference to me. Whether she's pregnant or not makes absolutely no difference to me."

I exasperated Judith more easily than in the past. I should like to know how I went from the status of being a brilliant writer to that of a self-centered professional.

I didn't see her again for two days. On two successive mornings, I went straight to the window when I woke up to see whether she had returned, whether her car was parked behind mine—which was not the case—then I looked out at the sort of hanging, inert rain that is characteristic of these parts, and I could see beyond it the dark mountains beneath a motionless, lowering sky, their outlines looming above the blanket of mist that hung over Labourd; I would have sighed with joy in other circumstances, but it annoyed me that she hadn't slammed the door for two days.

With the return of the sunshine—which, rather absurdly, had not shone during her absence—she reappeared in the garden. "Don't say a thing!" she uttered straightaway, raising her hand toward my mouth. "Whatever you do, don't say a thing!"

"Not even 'good morning'?" I asked.

It was probably nothing more than a minor tiff, a fairly mild starter compared to a complete separation of persons and assets, but the sample had left me with an unpleasant feeling.

The quality of my relationship with my daughter prompted me to act more prudently as far as my wife was concerned if I did not want to be left high and dry. That seemed quite clear to me. But there was further news concerning Alice, which she confided to me without further ado.

"She would like to spend some time at home. She's thinking of having her baby in Bayonne."

In the end I made it clear to her that I had no objection to that. She opened her mouth, but I put a finger to her lips. "Don't say a thing," I said. "Please. Don't say a thing."

I left it to her to inform Alice that I was happy for her to come—I even insisted that she did—and this new attitude on my part—conciliatory and affable—brought me some comfort, on the matrimonial front, over the following days.

"Do I have to keep an eye on your wife even when she is having dinner with you?" Jérémie smirked.

Five or six dinners in a row with me certainly seemed barely credible today. She would have to have a serious need of people around her, things going on, pregnant women, children, etc., to devote so much attention to me.

A man could easily lose both his wives and both his daughters. There was no doubt in my mind about this; it wasn't something I even wanted to discuss. I reckoned it was possible for a bombshell to fall in the exact same place as another, even if the probability was nil.

A few days before her death, the expression on A.-M.'s face altered. I suddenly became aware of it. I wanted to go and warn Jérémie, then I changed my mind.

It was almost like losing a girlfriend. No doubt we had met each other again far too late, and in difficult circumstances, but those three months spent together, those problems that we had delved into, those scars uncovered over time, those meals consumed on the run, those friendly visits, those favors done, the relationship we may have had in the past, etc., all this, and still more, had mattered a good deal. I had eventually forgotten that she had been involved in a relationship with a woman when I had gone to look her up in order to make inquiries about Alice's disappearance. Every life was like some terrifying journey, some mad race.

I was deeply moved and affected by her death. I had suggested to Jérémie that he take a few days off—I did my best to get him to find out whether this would pose any problem—but he did not think it was necessary to do so and merely performed his minimal duties in the evening, which he carried out wearing his appalling silicone gloves in my embarrassed presence, as I looked on in disbelief.

"Morphine helps a lot," she announced readily, although I was not able to determine whether she was referring to her own pain or the grief her son was causing her.

It was starting to get hot when she decided not to get up anymore. I rushed off to Castorama to buy her an electric fan before they sold out. On the last day, she was no longer really conscious, but on the previous day, when I switched on the fan for the first time, she let out a long sigh.

On the last day, I switched it off quickly, for she suddenly hunched up her body and complained about feeling very cold. It was as if she had shrunk, as if the skin on her face was nothing more than the translucent frame of a rather dull chrysalis, as if her eyes had become dark and were receding.

Glancing up, I saw that he was standing in the doorway and was observing the scene. From afar.

I motioned to him to come closer, trying to make him understand that if he wanted to catch his mother's last breath, he should not delay much longer. His eyes met mine for a moment, and then he walked away.

Flabbergasted, I leaped to my feet, knocked over my chair noisily, and took a few steps to stride across the living room and then the entrance hall, but the idiot was already far away, tearing off like a rocket with his dog into the pine forests and the heather. I went back and sat down. "I'm here," I said, stroking her shoulder, but she was dead.

I went outside again, in the scorching afternoon light. I shut the mosquito screen behind me.

I heard the first crickets of the summer at the cemetery, as the priest was adding a few words to a passage from the Gospel that he had read out in the warm air. I had taken charge of everything. The official papers. The undertakers. The church. I had been forced to forsake my novel for two entire days—which will seem of little consequence to the uninitiated, but the seriousness of this will be all too obvious to anyone who practices this trade. And the whole thing had killed me. It had inevitably reminded me of gloomy times. Having to deal with this burial from A to Z.

It was impossible to lay hands on Jérémie. I had had to

choose the coffin myself, choose the clothes from her drawers, choose the flowers, choose the tombstone, etc., because her son could not be found. Staggering.

I could not comprehend such indifference. I thought that if he had married Alice, they would have made quite a couple—had my life mattered any more as far as Alice was concerned? Certainly not. Not an ounce more.

The photograph had been taken just after 1968. I had long hair and wore bell-bottom trousers. I came across it in a drawer in her wardrobe as I was choosing the blouse and the few items of jewelry she would take with her into the hereafter. I did not know of the existence of this photo, whose colors had faded. For a moment I wondered how a photo of me came into her possession.

I never stopped glancing around furtively. The coffin was being lowered. I was beginning to give up hope. I moved forward to throw in my fistful of earth, then I stepped back. At that moment I caught sight of him, in the shade of a yew tree.

I immediately bent down low and wandered away so I could take him from the rear. I collared him. I raised my arm and hit him with the palm of my hand. An avalanche of resounding blows rained down on him—on his head, on his arms, on his back—which he protected himself against with difficulty, and some of them made him reel, such as the one that struck him on the ear and must have left him deaf on one side, for a while at least. Without my saying anything to him. Without my making the slightest comment. Without respite. I swooped on him like a windmill.

In the end, they overpowered me, they pinned me to the ground—they trained hard in this part of the world. I saw blue sky, distant, innocent clouds pinned to the firmament, and then Judith's face bent over me. She stroked my cheek and offered me her bottle of Evian.

This entire story—this tragic and scarcely credible, absolutely horrible sequence of events—resurfaced a year later, during a meal at the house of some friends, one of whom had heard tell that Jérémie was back in town.

Was it possible? Did he hope to start afresh with my wife? Was he going to try to kill himself again if he didn't get what he wanted? I noticed that everyone was staring at me.

"Does Judith know this?" I asked.

Apparently she didn't. The same person had come across Judith the previous day, leaving her house—we no longer lived under the same roof and we hardly ever spoke to one another—and there was nothing he had noticed in her behavior to suggest that she knew. "She'll find out eventually, one way or another," he said. "I believe he has de-cided to put his house up for sale." News carried so quickly in this town that there was always a slight buzz in the air.

Back at my house, I stayed sitting on my bed, in the darkness. Then the baby began crying and I lay down.

When I woke up the following day, he was crying again—I hoped that he had slept in the meantime. I went out to pick up the newspaper, in the dazzling June light.

"Jérémie is back," I announced as I walked into the kitchen.

Alice was sitting with her son in her arms and things did not seem to be going quite as either of them wished: the row with the babysitter, who had stormed out at the beginning of the weekend, had suddenly catapulted the mother and the child into a gloomy relationship.

She looked up at me. I didn't know whether I felt like eating eggs. Nor even whether I felt hungry.

"Do you want any eggs?" I asked her.

"Now there's someone who certainly knows what he wants," she giggled.

I shook my head and broke a few eggs into a pan. "I'm thinking of Judith. I tell myself that she hasn't deserved all this."

"She has a little, all the same."

"The boy's half crazy, she could have seen that, couldn't

she? It's quite obvious. Do you think I was surprised? Do you think I was surprised by what he did? Do you think that a guy who holds up a service station with a fully loaded shotgun has got all his wits about him?"

"Listen. He didn't threaten her."

"Totally agreed. He didn't force her. I totally agree. The fact remains, he's half crazy. Did you see what he did? Pity he bungled it."

I went upstairs to my study and shut the door. I remained seated in front of the telephone—an old model with an ebonite cord, which I used in order to protect me from brain cancer, which I feared like the plague.

Eventually, I rang Judith. While the phone was ringing at the other end, I held my breath and turned to look out of the window where the sky was indistinguishable from the sea, which was indistinguishable from the dunes where long grasses grew in the shape of feathers waving in the wind.

I was not expecting her to say anything and there was no lack of silence when I informed her of the reason for my call.

"Are you still there?"

"It's kind of you to warn me, Francis."

"If there's anything I can do, don't hesitate."

"It's all right. Don't worry about me."

"How's business? Are things going well?"

"Moderately. Congratulations on your book."

"Yes. I can't tell you how much good it's done me. It came at just the right time, of course, as you can imagine."

"I know, Francis. I can well imagine. I apologize. I'm deeply sorry."

"Don't talk nonsense. Listen. Look after yourself. That's all I ask. I want you to call me if anything goes wrong."

My hand was sweaty and my ear was burning when I hung up—and I stared at the handset with mixed feelings.

In the evening, after a particularly difficult working session due to events that had upset me, I bumped into Alice, freed of her baby but looking distraught, and clearly lost in her thoughts and various anxieties—unless, being an actress, she was meditating upon sorrow.

I went to the fridge. I suggested cooking some eggs. Dusk was falling, transforming the horizon into a blazing glow. In my case, I had been able to see the ray of green on various occasions—the last time at the very moment that I was putting the final period to my novel, which I reckoned meant that everything augured well.

"Or else, let's order a pizza," I said, "that's the easiest thing."

Then I sat down in an armchair with the books section and very soon began to boil inwardly, then to curse inwardly: this process was triggered weekly, each page being a source of anger, incredulity, despondency; each page fully deserving of being chucked into the wastepaper basket, were it not for a few authors, here and there, who, miraculously, really were worthy of interest; powerful, innovative, and uncompromising writers, who alone were worth the effort.

Since it was growing dark, I switched on a few lights. She returned, after having made endless telephone calls. She froze, for a brief second, listening in mild alarm, but the baby was not crying; it must have been the screech of a hawk or an owl hooting in the distance that was the cause of her anxiety.

"Listen. I've a problem getting a babysitter," she said, adopting a sullen expression.

"Yes, I know, I'm aware," I replied as I scanned the bestseller list.

"I need to go out for an hour. Is it all right if I'm away for an hour?"

I glanced at her, frowning.

"That's not part of our agreement."

"I haven't asked you for a single thing yet. Ever since I've been here."

"That's what we decided. It's one of the rules we introduced."

She lit a cigarette nervously. I perused the front page of the newspaper, which showed a column of tanks advancing in a cloud of dust. "Céline was wrong," I said. "It's not the Chinese who are going to invade us."

Jérémie's house had been empty for only a year, but it had a deserted look. This impression was mainly due to the garden, overrun by deadwood, debris, and branches brought down by the violent winds that had swept the coast over recent months, and by the hail, the thunderstorms, the lightning, or else by the frost that had ruined the bougainvillea I had planted when we moved in.

In front of the porch, the hydrangea bushes had grown enormously but had lost their color. The paint on the shutters had now flaked off completely and one could see the ash-colored wood underneath.

The placard advertising that it was for sale gave the name and telephone number of Judith's agency.

I switched on the ignition again and drove off.

Being without Roger's and Judith's help in these difficult times—not to even mention the chaotic and depressing forces that orchestrated the drunken course of the world—looking after the twins, once it was required of us again, turned into a virtual nightmare. I had begun a new book, which demanded firm discipline on my part, long periods of working in silence, calm, concentration, solitude, etc., which was precisely the opposite of what the girls had in store for me.

The problem was largely due to the babysitters who would let us down without warning to go and join their boyfriends or commit some misdeed or other that required their immediate dismissal—such as the latest one, who had managed to scald the baby the shade of a lobster.

All of a sudden, I had to do the shopping, take the girls to the supermarket, find things to interest them, read books such as *Bridget Jones's Diary* to them—"Why bother?" I asked myself—or dash off to Bayonne to buy them DVDs and Petit Bateau T-shirts.

One way or another, my days were disrupted. This was not what I had agreed with Alice. She could move into the house. Period. Nothing else. Move into the house, period. As long as she left me in peace. Nothing else.

"Very well, I know that. And what do you expect me to do? They're your granddaughters, you know. It's not two arms I need, it's four."

The baby was wriggling about on her lap, ready to start crying again. His two sisters were breathing down my neck, waiting to drag me around the shops in town to look for a swimming costume.

I leaned down to whisper into her ear: "Call Roger. Explain the situation to him. Ask him to come down and take them away on this occasion."

"Listen. Don't involve yourself with that. Let Judith sort it out. Don't be ridiculous."

"I'm not in the mood to run a day nursery at the moment. Isn't that obvious?"

I ended the day in the Nouvelles Galeries—they had forgotten their shampoo and wanted to choose a suntan lotion.

Dusk was falling. Judith was shutting up the agency— her knees bent, holding the door handle with one hand,

and turning the key in a lock at the bottom of the door with the other.

The girls jumped up to clasp her round the neck. As for me, I took advantage of their hugging to take a close look at her. She had a worried expression.

"You shouldn't be doing this," I said.

"Selling houses is my job. That's how I earn my living."

We walked down toward the casino and strolled beside the sea, coming across a few surfers—among the hardiest ones probably—who were getting ready to spend the night in their tiny minivan, equipped with a bed, a portable gas stove, and a rack for surfboards.

Judith was walking with her head down, like a robot. I wanted to tell her that her decision had infuriated me; that no serious reflection could result in the conclusion that she had any reason to see Jérémie again, or speak to him, after the gruesome trick he had played on her.

She was unsure. They had simply spoken on the telephone.

"You're unsure? Have I understood correctly? Do you think there's anything to be unsure about? Have I heard correctly? You're unsure? Listen, it's quite simple. See him again and I wash my hands of what happens. See him again and you'll regret it. And don't say I didn't tell you so."

We stopped in front of the ice-cream parlor. I missed not living with her anymore. When I thought about it, I figured that she had done to me what I had done to Johanna and that a sort of natural justice was thereby established, one that might enable us to start again at the beginning, but this was not the case. The two things were not comparable. I wouldn't have been able to explain why, but the two things were not comparable.

I turned my gaze in the direction of the Avenue de l'Impératrice. "I should like to know the reason why the dome of St. Alexander Nevsky has been changed from blue to gray," I remarked, to change the conversation. "Hasn't anyone made a fuss?"

Less than a fortnight later, the house had not been sold, but she was sleeping with Jérémie again. The last thing I could have imagined.

Two or three voices were raised, criticizing me for having created the circumstances for their meeting by paying Jérémie to follow her. But of course they were. Naturally.

Alice was first. It wasn't enough for her to intrude upon me. Her own wreckage of a marriage wasn't enough for her. I threatened to crack her skull open if she opened her mouth again. Or even to chuck her out, but she could not stop herself voicing her opinion about the way I dealt with my relationship with my wife, showing me just how badly I had handled things with her, just how much I now lacked dignity by involving myself in a matter that no longer concerned me.

She forgot that her own marriage had also collapsed, that her affairs had not had the anticipated piquancy—the newspapers were going on about her romantic idylls with someone who looked the spitting image of Shia LaBeouf—she forgot that she was feeling a little lost and incapable of soothing an infant who burst into tears the moment she picked him up, she forgot that she was here, under my roof, in my house, due to some kind of miracle after the way she had behaved toward me.

"You're wrong to think that I wouldn't throw you out. It wouldn't cause me any problem."

"I'm sure of that. Mama was right. Mama was right when she said that the more one delved into you, the frostier you became."

I grabbed her by the wrist. "What are you talking about? I got on perfectly well with her. Don't say such things. Don't invent such nonsense. Don't overstep the mark, Alice."

I let go of her; I pushed her arm away abruptly.

"Do you think we didn't used to talk about you, perhaps?" she replied.

I stepped outside. "Do you think the fact that you were a writer frightened us? Do you think that it impressed us?"

I walked away. "Do you think we didn't know who you were?"

She added something else, but I was already far away.

Once again, I walked as far as Hendaye. The weather was fine and the beaches were still empty. I went and had dinner at Fontarabie, then I got drunk with some friends I met there. The wife of one of them kept her hand on my thigh for a good part of the evening. Her husband wanted to know what my next book was about. And she kept on saying to him: "Oh, come on now, leave Francis alone. You can see you're annoying him. Oh, come on now, leave Francis alone with your questions. You can see he doesn't want to answer you. Oh, come on . . ." Etc.

Lucie-Anne and Anne-Lucie had been putting on their mother's makeup. I looked up from my computer screen when I heard Alice's yells. "The poor girl is at her wit's end," I said to myself, returning to the job in hand and trying to rediscover the particular rhythm I was trying to impress on a sentence that had been holding up the entire novel for a good twenty minutes; I had this habit, when things weren't working out for me and in order to alarm myself even more, of turning on the timer on my cell phone.

But she was screeching much too loudly for me to be able to compose the slightest thing.

Touching her makeup was certainly the most serious offense one could commit in the little world of theirs, and the girls, ever since they had set eyes on this world, had been given ample warning. When I arrived, Alice was now wanting to know what had got into them, and the silence of the twins, who said nothing and were rooted to the spot, their heads sunk into their shoulders and their eyes lowered, made their mother shout even louder.

I stayed to admire the spectacle for a moment, but the yelling caused me to flee just as surely as the faces of certain authors do; it cannot be overstated just how much a writer resembles his own style, and how blatant this is.

What a fool I'd been to let her into my house, I told myself, while glass was shattering upstairs. That's what happened when you hadn't been filming for six months.

I made myself a bowl of fat-free fromage frais for my afternoon snack. If it went on like that, she would have no voice left and her daughters would have perforated eardrums.

I didn't know how long my patience would hold out at this rate; Alice did not enjoy a great deal of credit in my books, nor did she have my entire sympathy. I had taken pity on her for a fleeting second and she had stormed off before I could finish formulating the details of my strict conditions. And instead of things improving, they got worse. I was entitled to some kind of nervous breakdown upstairs. I knew that often—and even in the majority of cases—bringing up a family meant cries, blood, and tears, but was I going to feel sorry for her because of this? Was I going to sympathize with the harshness of her fate?

I made a few pieces of toast, which I spread with raspberry jam. And I was about to bite into a slice when I noticed the twins, hesitant and keeping a low profile, holding each other's hand, their eyes glued to the object I held between two fingers, topped with such a lovely red, ruby color.

I held out the plate to them so that if they liked these things with raspberry jam on them, they could help themselves. I put down the one I was intending to eat myself, before they bit my hand off.

I advised them to keep out of harm's way until the evening, to find themselves something serious to do, such as watching *Gone with the Wind* or starting *Sense and Sensibility*—which I strongly recommended personally—which would allow me time to do a little more work, and afterward I would come and see whether there was anything they needed, such as getting something to eat should their mother forget that she had two little girls to feed; they could trust me, I would not abandon them. *South Park?* Of course they could watch *South Park*—I didn't even know what they were talking about.

◆

Passing by her bedroom, I could hear her sobbing quietly. In the old days, I would have knocked on her door to see whether everything was all right.

She considered that my behavior toward her was not worthy of a father. She told me that she would soon have been there for six months and that in those six months she had seen how cold I could be, she had been able to observe how far my indifference could go. "It's even worse than I feared," she told me.

She was wrong to think I did it deliberately.

"If it's so as to punish me, you know . . ."

"It's not to punish you, Alice. There's nothing I can do. There was probably a bit of that, in the very beginning, but it didn't last very long. Resuscitation had not been possible. I'd be delighted to inform you of the opposite, you know."

"I'm telling you. I know of no one who is capable of such spitefulness toward his own daughter. Absolutely no one."

I stood up. I was much more concerned about the fact that Judith had allowed Jérémie back into her bed; he was scarcely out of his convalescence and now had long hair, according to my sources. The story was already provoking a good deal of laughter.

One evening I paid for a woman whom I brought back to the house. I imagined her to be a prostitute, but as we walked along I realized—in spite of the effect the alcohol had on the functioning of my brain—that she worked at the central post office.

I guided her, somehow or other, to my study, walking through the dark and silent house with a finger vaguely on my lips and an arm around her neck.

I needed to unwind. When she wasn't busy pointing out my faults and my failings, Alice made some telephone calls that depressed her still further owing to the ups and downs of this roller-coaster profession. She threatened to change agents, to return to the theater, to bring a lawsuit against the firm that supplied her with babysitters; I could hear her pacing back and forth, slamming cupboard doors, wailing occasionally, or even stamping her foot.

She made the atmosphere unbearable. I hadn't paid for my ticket in order to have a grandstand view of the life of one of those girls one saw more or less everywhere. I hadn't asked for anything. What did it matter that I should have succumbed to the panic of living alone or yielded to some sort of instinctive fatherly weakness? I hadn't asked for anything. Whatever the situation.

She had interrupted me in the middle of the afternoon on the pretext that she had suddenly run out of milk for the baby. Which was the reason why the child, at that very moment, began kicking up a terrible fuss.

"You have the look of a man who has had a tough day," the woman who came up to me at the bar had said. I had offered her a few drinks and, when my head began to loll on the counter, she had stroked my neck.

I didn't turn on the light because a bright, ash-colored, powdery, and absolutely wonderful moonlight was bathing this room that normally witnessed me toiling and wringing my hands.

I undid my trousers and took them off with the greatest difficulty in the world—innocent that I was, convinced that the trials of the day have an end, that sufficient unto the day is the evil thereof, etc.

"I'm saving up to buy myself a Vespa," she confided to me as she folded her clothes over a chair.

Alice slammed the door so violently as she went out that a postcard I had had framed—Hemingway writing to say thank you for the anchovies—fell off the wall and the glass shattered into a thousand pieces on the wooden floor, while the slamming of the door continued to reverberate so loudly in my head that I remained momentarily stunned—my eyes closed, my underpants down to my knees, my hands clasped on the ample buttocks of the postal worker—as if struck by lightning.

I withdrew from my partner, who was taken aback for a moment, but as far as I was concerned the whole thing was ruined and my erection dwindled almost immediately.

The post office woman pulled up her knickers nonchalantly. She had quite pretty legs, milky white skin, and a nicely rounded belly, but it was too late, and all I really wanted to do was to have a drink and recover my spirits.

◆

I received Alice's pledge—that henceforth she would never address another word to me—serenely.

I knew that it wouldn't be the cause of my death.

Did I not already have one foot in the next world? I often thought of this following my separation from Judith—and Alice's extreme bad moods, which in themselves were unimportant, only added to my vexation. Of the four women who had given meaning to my existence, two were dead, one had left me, and the remaining one refused to speak to me.

I thanked heaven for having given me literature. I thanked literature for having given me a job to do, for having provided for the needs of my family, for having let me experience the thrill of success, for having punished me, for having made me stronger, and I thanked it today for the hand it still proffered to me, but would it be sufficient from now on? Would literature maintain the role it had played for much longer, as far as I was concerned? Now that I was alone, now that the dust was settling again.

I scarcely went out anymore, in any case. I had soon grown tired of those evenings when kindly souls placed me opposite the obligatory single woman—wearing a low-cut dress, inclined to blush, and either silent or completely hysterical—who was supposed to suit me down to a T. I had had my fill of sympathetic looks, of ineffectual embraces, of smiles of consternation, of endless discussions as to the reasons that could have propelled Judith into the arms of a totally uncontrollable twenty-six-year-old lad; I had built up a considerable stock of encouragements, of comforting words, of invitations telling me that I was not to feel awkward and to call by, night or day, if things were going badly, if I was in a gloomy mood. How could I have explained just how unbearable I found this concern, just how much it upset me?

It was not in the least surprising that I should not feel any better today. Added to the fiasco of the previous day—extremely frustrating, extremely unpleasant—were the expressions of disgust on Alice's face; she pretended to believe that I had picked up some tropical disease—possibly a venereal one—and she walked away from me as the twins looked on in bewilderment.

"One *knocks* at a door," I said after two days of silence. "One knocks and one waits for permission to enter. When one has a minimum of good manners. No? It's the proper way to behave. Is it too much to ask of you? Haven't I the right to some *private* space in this house? I am in my own home, I believe. Listen. I'm going to tell you something. I don't want to have people living in my house who sulk at me. It's only human, isn't it?"

Before the anger came pure rage; her expression registered surprise and total amazement. Then she grabbed her daughters by the hand and immediately dashed upstairs.

I waited for a few moments, leafing through a literary magazine; my comment concerning the astonishing resemblance between a writer's physical features and his handwriting (the same adjectives applied to them exactly) was borne out daily (give me the photograph of a writer and I will tell you how he writes). After which, since there was no sign of the girls, and because I could no longer hear them, I decided to go and see.

"Are you packing your bags?" I asked.

Half a dozen suitcases were well and truly open, as well as the windows, the cupboard doors, the different drawers they had at their disposal—which I had already emptied once, and which she had filled again—and everything seemed to be in a huge mess.

Sitting on the edge of the bed, keeping their mouths shut, the twins glanced at me sadly while their mother, conspicuously turning her back to me, continued to fold their clothes, her jaws clenched.

I detected a sort of confusion in her movements, however. There was clothing everywhere, almost as if a typhoon had passed through.

"I am sorry to have a sexual life," I said.

She stopped in her tracks without turning around.

Then she slowly got on with what she was doing.

I observed that the little girls were staring at me intently.

"Think about it," I said to her.

◆

I watched her suddenly fling her arms around my neck. Weeping silently on my shoulder. I thought it would never stop; the light of the setting sun accentuated this feeling. "I'm sorry," she sobbed. "Oh forgive me, Papa, I'm sorry." A kind of continuous prayer that seemed to come out of a dream.

I patted her back. I laid my hand on her head. I waited until she had finished, allowing myself to be distracted by the breeze in the curtains above her shoulder, which reminded me of a playful and invisible young animal.

One gray, very windy morning, I was in the kitchen listening to the radio and grilling some toast, as the coffee seeped through the filter and the world's news trickled out, when all of a sudden, looking up, I spotted Jérémie.

He was standing on the other side of the road, by the edge of the dunes. For a second, seeing how he had aged, how he had become wizened in a year and turned gray, I stood as if dumbstruck.

I stepped back from the window. I knew that he had been between life and death, that the bullet had missed his heart by a few millimeters, I knew about it, of course—who didn't?—but I did not expect to see an apparition, a veritable ghost. What a shock! I'd bet he wasn't going to start picking quarrels around the place anymore—unless he was going to select the very pale and the very puny.

Having recovered from my surprise, I leaned out of the window again to see whether he was still there. Whether the wind hadn't blown him away, mistaking him for a scarecrow.

It was difficult for me to go and confront the person who had stolen my wife—even if it was the price I paid for my own neglect—but he just stood there in the wind, his hands dug into his pockets, his shoulders hunched, his eyes downcast, and I knew he wasn't going to budge.

I went to open my front door. I glanced around me quickly. I beckoned to him. As I watched him draw near, I could feel all my anger, all my resentment vanish into thin air, without explanation, as if by magic, and I imagined, no doubt rather clumsily, that when a woman's waters broke she must feel as I felt at that moment.

We stood there in the doorway for an instant, in the draft, face to face.

"I wanted to tell you that I was here," he eventually announced.

I paused. "I'd been told. It's a small town."

He nodded. He seemed exhausted.

"Alice is living here at present," I said. "With the girls."

"Ah."

"It's best that you don't come in."

"I wanted to tell you . . ."

"Good heavens."

"Listen . . ."

Behind him, long gray clouds were sailing across the sky

from east to west, flying along the Spanish coast like strange and somber troop carriers, and yet the visibility was so clear that one could see as far as Cape Machichaco.

"No, you listen to me."

"I didn't mean to."

"But you did."

"I swear to you I didn't."

"Good heavens."

"Not on your life."

"But you did."

Some seagulls that were flying against the wind above the road cried as they began a series of loop-the-loops.

"Good heavens."

"You were . . ."

"Oh good heavens."

"Thanks to you . . ."

"Shut up."

"I'm cursed."

"Stop it."

I could hear the twins coming downstairs. We exchanged a final glance, then I asked him to leave. His head dropped once more, and his hair fell into his eyes. Suddenly, he tried to take my hand, but I pulled it back in time.

I waited until he was on the road again before releasing the door handle and went about my business once more.

◆

"Who was it?"

"It was Jérémie."

"Who was it?"

"It was Jérémie."

"You're joking. I hope you're joking. Jérémie? But what did he want?"

"Well, would you believe, he didn't tell me. It was very odd. In any case, he didn't look very steady on his legs yet."

"You amaze me."

I couldn't do very much for him. I hoped that if his mother could see me, from her cushion of white clouds on high, she wouldn't have held it too much against me. I hoped so. But the situation had become impossible ever since her son had become my wife's lover. My feelings had become impossible, too.

As soon as I relinquished the private domain of the novel I was working on—which I naturally had to devote most of my efforts to—these bitter feelings came over me, swamped me, and I found it difficult to rid myself of them. So it was that, not having followed the latest developments in the Alice-Roger relationship—I had no idea where they'd got to exactly—I discovered to my surprise, a few days later, that he was here, recently arrived from the airport, looking vaguely miserable, and that they had decided to have it out with one another.

When I asked Alice where he had been, she replied: "Don't get mixed up in that. Don't be unpleasant to him. All he did was to obey me."

"Obey you?"

"Yes, obey me. Sorry."

"I'm sorry," I said, "he hasn't just obeyed you. He's been carrying on this game under my very eyes, day after day, knowing that I was dead worried, listening to me groaning and allowing me to believe that I'd lost you forever. Obey you? He can roast in hell."

She sighed briefly. "Tell me, but what is it we have to do, ultimately, in order to hear no more about this business?"

I shrugged my shoulders and kept them raised to indicate my ignorance in the matter, and my subsequent confusion, while she did an about-face.

My view was that everyone was wrong about everyone else. No need to be a genius. Therefore, how could living together have turned out to be a simple matter? How could one have prevented entire nations from sinking into madness when they were founded on ignorance and error?

"Can you make quite sure he hasn't got a gun? Judith? Do you think you could do that? Do you think you could look into it? Do you think you could stop imagining that these things only happen to other people? Could you open your eyes for a moment? Could you open your eyes just for a second and make sure that he hasn't got a damned gun at his disposal?"

While I was in my study, seated on the arm of the famous sofa, gazing out of the window, I lavished my advice on Judith over the telephone—wondering whether she was still capable of acting discerningly—and at the same time I was watching Alice and Roger down below, in the garden, busy sorting out their life together.

Alice had landed an important role in a French television series and she had realized immediately that she would have to come to an arrangement with Roger if she was to pursue her career instead of spending her days looking after children. I could not hear what they were saying, but she was waving her arms around in an impassioned way.

"How could I have let you do that, you and Jérémie?" I sighed. "How could I not have prevented it by force? By withdrawing from the race I was not acting in your best interests. Quite simply, I should not have listened to you. I should have locked you in the cellar and blocked my ears."

Then there was this spectacle: Anne-Lucie on Alice's lap and Lucie-Anne on Roger's lap. The sky was blue and streaked with plumes of smoke made by airplanes.

"I know him better than you do. You know that very well. I spent days and days with him. Wait. I went to pick him up when he came out of prison. Why do you make me repeat that? I'm not asking you to give me a speech, I'm asking you to make sure he doesn't have a gun. Do as I say. Sleeping with him shouldn't make you forget what he's capable of. How many times do I have to go on telling you that?"

Now it was the other way around: Anne-Lucie on Roger's lap and Lucie-Anne on Alice's lap. The sky was completely blue, with white plumes of smoke made by airplanes.

"I know I'm unpleasant, I'm well aware. I don't want to be pleasant this morning. I couldn't explain why. Am I writing? Of course, I'm writing. I'm lucky to be writing. If you are listening to me at this moment, if you have me on the other end of the line, it's because I am writing. That's why I'm still breathing. It's not thanks to you."

This sofa had withstood the decades to attest to the fact that writing was the last thing left. That there was nothing else afterward. Every second of July I raised a glass in its company.

"The third time he'll get it right. I'm sorry. Do you hear me? It's not that I want to frighten you, Judith, but I know this boy. Good God, do I know this boy."

I was more angry with her for her stupidity than for her infidelity; I would also have preferred to have a rival who was a little older, which would have made the situation a little less painful, a little less obscene, rather than this loathsome triangle that we made up; having my wife snatched from me by a twenty-six-year-old guy who looked barely twenty was something I had never imagined could happen to me. I noticed two paparazzi in the dunes, draped with two enormous cameras. Good old Roger. There was someone who saw things in the long term. The very opposite of Judith. Over the sea, the sun seemed to be crackling. She was silent on the other end of the line.

"It's your friend speaking to you," I said before hanging up.

Alice had a far more clear-cut view of the matter than I did. She reckoned that Judith was pathetic. I nodded vaguely. I watched her as she dressed her baby and I reflected on the extent to which everything had dissipated between us, how deep the wound was, the extent to which I had lost her. It was puzzling and terrible at the same time.

"You know that very well. I feel ashamed for her. It's ridiculous. He looks like her son. It's like a mother sleeping with her son."

She was a little on edge, for we had run out of babysitters for the day. Roger had taken the twins to the beach. The baby was whining, expecting better.

She glanced at me. "Don't you agree? She's a bit on the old side, isn't she?"

Alice and Judith had always been on good terms. Never excellent. I had had time to read a good deal about the re-action of a daughter to her father's remarrying, and I knew that this was delicate, uncertain ground, liable to create tension.

"That's not the problem."

"They call it the male menopause. That's just what it's all about. Don't stress yourself. Forget it."

"Should I stop being concerned about what happens to her? Behave as if she were a stranger?"

"I don't know. But as far as I'm concerned, I don't like people making you look ridiculous."

So she was not exactly glad to see Jérémie move back into his house—and Judith paying him a visit—less than five minutes later. "It's not good for your career or for mine," she told me. "It doesn't make a very good impression, you know."

Had I not known for a fact that my daughter had no sense of humor, I would have immediately thought that she was joking.

"She's right," said Roger, without looking up from his newspaper. "Very bad for both your images."

Very well. I decided to do without their company in the future.

And so with the summer approaching, in spite of Alice's various entreaties—in every tone of voice and on every level of pitch, from tears to prayers, from flattery to threats—I agreed willingly to have the little girls to stay for vacations, but neither her nor Roger. I did not want either of them in my home any longer. The page had been turned.

Alice considered me insufferable and let it be known that I had become an irascible old writer, temperamental, narrow-minded, inflexible, and sometimes spiteful, capable of shutting his door on his own daughter, of forbidding her entry into his house. Elderly writers often became perfectly unbearable, she claimed, and I was well on the way. I was just about able to look after a dog and wander around a large, empty house, churning out page after page. An old misanthropic animal.

Very well. I thanked her for the publicity she was providing me with, on the basis that it was better to be spoken about badly than not at all. My agent would not be the one to contradict me.

In the hour that followed, I called Judith at the agency and informed her of the new arrangements that I had made with respect to the unwanted couple. The sky was bright. I added that time was hurrying on and that it was our responsibility to make arrangements regarding the arrival of the twins as soon as possible.

I was proud of standing firm, of not having yielded to my fatherly duties—and yet paradoxically, it had not been so difficult. Possibly nothing else, I told myself, would seem difficult from now on.

◆

I prepared for her arrival. I aired her bedroom for two whole days before she came. I took on a Portuguese cleaning woman. I arranged for the Thai gardener to come.

I was very pleased with this experiment in communal life that Judith and I were going to conduct during these holidays, and with this provisional, temporary return home. Very impatient, very anxious.

I had spoken to her during the course of the previous month, but I hadn't seen her. She looked to me to be in good shape as I watched her get out of her car and then walk across the garden in her white suit and blue high-heeled shoes, now completely recovered from her wound—the bullet had pierced the side of her abdomen, but already there was virtually no trace of it. I thought her impressive and resilient.

I carried her two suitcases—each of them sixty pounds or so—upstairs to her bedroom.

I wanted to say a few words on this occasion.

"Thank you," I said to her.

Anne-Lucie and Lucie-Anne rushed over toward me the moment they arrived, as soon as they saw the Petit Bateau bag that I was holding, with a knowing smile on my face, under my arm—we had had a particular discussion in which they had informed me of their liking for basic things, of their fondness for cotton, like their grandmother.

I was in an excellent mood. Judith and I had spent a simple but excellent evening together—both of us very much determined, of course, that it should be thus, but nevertheless, there was no deception, nothing that convinced us we were yet able to sit down opposite one another, each of us was free to get up and declare that it was impossible, with the best will in the world, there was no deception—an excellent evening for both of us, which we concluded in the mild air of the garden in the company of the fireflies.

Alice's head was covered in a scarf and she was wearing enormous dark glasses; she had not got anything in Cannes, although she was in the running for a prize for acting.

"I'm not going to get down on my knees to you," she said, gritting her teeth, after drawing me to one side. "I'm certainly not going to throw myself at your feet."

I smiled at her with total sincerity. "Let's keep what's still left to be kept," I said. "Let's not be too reckless."

The twins were waving at me to tell me that their bags could be seen on the conveyor belt.

Alice's head dropped and she sank into a frosty silence for a while. "Why her?" she blurted out eventually in a voice that was unrecognizable.

I waited for her to raise her head, for her to look me in the eyes, but she didn't move. "For a thousand and one reasons, Alice," I replied.

◆

Certainly, Judith and I had no intention of getting back together, each of us being aware that we could not go return
to the past and repair our mistakes. But that did not prevent
us from doing favors for one another, from time to time,
as the days and months went by. There was nothing like
living on good terms. Nothing like an ending that offered a
glimpse of light. Nothing like an ending that bathed the far
shore of the novel in undeserved sweetness.

Well, it didn't take very much for that fine summer, that
soothing feeling I no longer believed in, that haven, to be
plunged into unreal and bloody chaos.

So it was that a few months earlier, at the height of a
crisis that Alice's difficulties, among other things, only
made worse—it seemed as if my honor was at stake, and my
honor appeared to be the thing my daughter valued more
than anything else in the world these days—I had eventually decided to—well—put the knife into the wound and, as
the stern and flinty evening drew on, I set off.

A warm inland breeze was brewing, blowing toward
the sea, clouds were unraveling over the ocean, which was
covered in foam, etc.

Pale and gloomy, I had arrived at Jérémie's door. Pinecones were rolling across the terrace, the wind was sough-
ing in the branches, which were creaking and cracking, the
horizon was fading and flickering like a pale altar candle,

the porch lighting emanated from a 1900-style lantern that squeaked as it swayed in the gusting wind.

Usually, it was A.-M. whom I saw framed in this doorway, it was she whom I used to visit, she to whom I came and confided my sorrows—and had a drink—but A.-M. had left us and I experienced a shock at seeing Judith on the doorstep—even though I was expecting to find her there.

I noticed that she was holding a glass in her hand and that her ears were slightly red.

"Having red ears, in this situation, seems entirely normal," I said as I sat down. "Your cheeks are, too. Entirely normal."

She lowered her gaze. "Jérémie should be arriving shortly."

"What? Very well. I'm not in a hurry."

She poured me a glass of wine. I crossed my legs.

I uncrossed them.

"I've plenty of time," I said after a few minutes.

I looked at her for a long while, then I asked her whether she couldn't control herself or whether she had gone mad, all the while leaning over toward her and asking her to refill my glass.

"Both, I think," she replied as she opened a second bottle.

I had rarely seen her drunk. It reminded me of some particularly happy or depressing times we had known during those twelve years of living together and I experienced a moment of genuine nostalgia.

Judith had not replaced Johanna and she had, no doubt, chosen a less brutal way of leaving me, but it was proving to be fairly painful all the same.

Time and distance were the enemy. Day after day, the more Johanna's image faded in my mind, the more I had idealized her, the more I had endowed her with all the virtues in the world. No woman could compare with this infernal machine. As far as I was concerned, anyway, there had been nothing I could do about it. Trying to be reasonable had been to no avail.

I glanced around me. "Did you tidy this house?"

"Here? Of course not."

"Ah. Very well."

"Oh my God."

"What?"

"Oh my God."

"Of course. What did you expect?"

I drained my glass and started to turn around as she slumped to the carpet. I stood in front of her.

"Alice was right. This meeting is absurd. Don't say it isn't. Where is he, are we allowed to know?"

Once again, my gaze was drawn to the photograph of Jérémie's father, on the mantelpiece—the man was still posing in his vest and shorts in front of his racing bike—and I did not find it strange that this man, with the shifty eyes and a vacant smile, should be at the source of a whole mass of problems that we were encountering here.

"The meat from Grisons? Of course I like it. I've lived in

Switzerland. But let's be clear: I've not come here to drink an aperitif. Judith. Don't start frightening me. Be careful. We're not going to leave one another shaking hands, I assure you."

"He's spent the afternoon making you a blueberry tart."

"I don't believe you."

"I think he really likes you. Really a lot. You can go and look in the oven, if you don't believe me."

I went and sat down again.

"I'd do better to get the hell out of here," I said after further consideration. I shook my head and then I got to my feet. I looked at the oven as I passed by and the tart was there right enough, I could smell it—and I could see at a glance that he had used my recipe.

Once outside, I breathed long and deeply.

I went back indoors.

"You weren't looking for anything? You weren't looking for anything? How can that be, Judith? *You weren't looking for anything?*" She tried to hold my gaze, but her own eventually subsided.

He had parked in the lane almost one hour later. Judith had felt much better after having been sick—*after* often having

had a taste for absolution—and she had just emptied a
bottle of mineral water when we heard him crashing into
the garbage cans that stood on the corner of the pavement.
As I listened, despite the wind, I could hear a few snatches
of music—and I seemed to recognize Jimi Hendrix singing
"All Along the Watchtower."

"What's he doing?" she asked.

"He's still sitting at the wheel. He's drinking a beer. I
wonder whether he's seen me."

We went outside. I walked across the garden in the
bright moonlight, then, as I was leaning over the door, pas-
senger's side, the car lurched forward and stopped a few
yards farther on. I chose to laugh about it and I stood up
straight. "Very funny!" I said.

As he went by, I was able to see his swollen face and the
cans of beer on the seat.

"What have you done this time?" I sighed as I walked
over toward the car again. "Who's been beating you up this
time, you stupid idiot?"

The car lurched forward once again. "Please don't do
that!" I yelled. His dog jumped out through the back window and started to leap around me. "We're supposed to
have a talk, Jérémie," I said as I put my hand on the car
door. "I haven't got time to play ga—" He almost ripped it
off with a burst of the accelerator.

"OK," I said, raising my hands in the air and turning
away. "I give up."

I picked Judith up on the way, grabbing her by the

elbow, as Jérémie swerved around to draw level with us.

"Hey!" he shouted.

I didn't answer, I didn't pay him the slightest attention. I held Judith firmly as I walked away, for fear that a moment's weakness might cause her to go back to her young lover again, but she offered only slight resistance.

"Hey!" he yelled again, braking sharply as we turned into the garden.

A deafening blast of gunfire froze us to the spot. Judith's eyes met mine. I was no angrier with her than I was angry with myself, quite honestly, but so much stupidity on our part, so much naïveté, so much thoughtlessness, so much foolhardiness as well, was astonishing. Jérémie had a gun in his hand. This same boy who had held up a service station, who had slashed his veins, who had shot himself full in the chest, that boy there, that Jérémie there, and no one else, had a gun in his hands once again and I reckoned he was completely drunk. I cursed between my teeth.

He shot out of his car like a man possessed and charged straight for us. His T-shirt was torn, his face was in a pitiful state, the bridge of his nose was gashed, his eye was black, bloated, and shiny—I reckoned he had probably suffered the biggest thrashing he had ever had since taking up this sport. Behind him, a few distant flashes of lightning lit up the peaks of the Trois Couronnes.

He fell to his knees in front of Judith like a wretched sinner before the Blessed Mother. I could foresee some extremely awkward moments ahead if he embarked upon this path—he would have to discover that throwing yourself at the feet of a woman did not guarantee anything. It was one of those dreadful lessons in life, according to Western customs.

A second burst of gunfire then rang out and we were spattered, she and I, with blood and other more solid substances. Jérémie fell backward. Then, so, too, did Judith, who, opening wide her sorrowful eyes, discovered that she happened to have been on the wrong trajectory.